AL

Tommy & Evelyn Christie Mysteries

Murder at the Manor

Murder at the Village Fete

Murder in the Churchyard

Murder at the Wedding Chapel

Murder at Rochester Park

Murder at the Seaside

Murder at Docere House

Murder at Killeven Castle (coming soon)

The Martha Miller Mysteries

Poison at the Village Show

Daggers at the Country Fair

Death at Lovers' Leap

The West Cliffe Bay Cosy Mysteries

Murder & Cappuccino (prequel introducing the series)

Murder & Lemon Cheesecake (coming soon)

MURDER AT DOCERE HOUSE

A 1920S COZY MYSTERY

A TOMMY & EVELYN CHRISTIE MYSTERY
BOOK 9

CATHERINE COLES

INSPIRED PRESS LIMITED

Editor: Paula & Terry Grundy

Cover Design: Sally Clements

eBook ISBN: 9781915126245

Paperback ISBN: 9781915126252

Large Print Hardback ISBN: 9781915126276

CAST OF CHARACTERS

Main Characters

Tommy Christie - The Seventh Earl of Northmoor, former police officer

Evelyn Christie - Policewoman during the Great War, Tommy's wife

The Family

Lady Isabelle Harriet Emily Christie – Tommy & Evelyn's daughter

Lady Emily Christie - Tommy's great-aunt

Hessleham Hall Staff

Albert Tomlinson – Estate Manager's assistant & chauffeur

Nora Tomlinson – Nanny

School Staff

Julia Davenport – Headmistress of Docere House

Ralph Gower – Science master

Bertie Adams – Ralph Gower's assistant

Francis Galbraith – Maths master at Docere House

Clarissa Cambridge – Julia's assistant
Edwin Miller – Elderly schoolmaster
Gilbert Wellesley – Student at Docere House
Nanny Bunting – Julia's secretary
Frank Mitchell – Head groom at Docere House
Daisy – maid at Docere House

Others

Detective Inspector Andrews - Senior detective from York
Detective Sergeant Montgomery - Junior detective
Dr Joseph Brady – GP

1

North Yorkshire – October 1923

"Are we nearly there?" Evelyn Christie looked at her husband with barely disguised impatience as their driver carefully wended his way through country lanes. She was all-too-well aware that each mile took her farther away from home.

"Were you always in such a hurry to get to school, darling?"

Evelyn gave him a sidelong glance. "You know very well I'm not in a hurry to get to Docere House. I am, however, keen to get home to our daughter."

"We left Hessleham Hall precisely fifteen minutes ago. Isabelle won't even realise we are gone. She will be perfectly happy with Nanny."

"I know she will be all right." Evelyn bit her lip,

which suggested she didn't quite believe her own words.

"Don't you trust Nora?"

Evelyn blinked and forced a smile to her lips. "You know I do. There's no one, other than family, that I trust more."

Nora Tomlinson had worked at Hessleham Hall as a kitchen maid for several years and was well known to Evelyn. She had carried on working in the kitchen even after she married the butcher's boy, Albert. However, when she became pregnant, he insisted she give up work. Evelyn could scarcely believe the boy, who had been terrified of the butcher he worked for, had grown into a man who capably ran his own household.

"That is a very sensible response." Tommy nodded towards their driver. "Considering her husband is currently driving us to Docere House."

"Oh Tommy." Evelyn elbowed her husband playfully. "You are always so keen to make light of everything."

"Not always." His lips thinned and Evelyn recalled the kidnapping of Josephine, Tommy's cousin's child, earlier that year. "Though you must admit it was a rather inspired suggestion of Aunt Em's that Nora become the children's nanny."

"Yes." Evelyn placed a hand over Tommy's and smiled up at him. "It has worked out perfectly for all of us."

Nora cared for her own child as well as Josephine, and Isabelle. Meanwhile, her husband, Albert, was no longer the butcher's boy but helped Tommy and Jack Partridge, the estate manager, to run Hessleham Hall. He also doubled as a driver now that Tommy was keen to use his new motorcar as often as possible. Although Evelyn knew the vehicle meant they could travel much faster, she still much preferred the steady, reassuring sound of a horse's hooves on the road rather than the roaring of a car's engine.

"You do know it wouldn't have been proper for us to bring Isabelle with us," Tommy said as though he could read her mind, which, after so many years together, he probably could.

"I know," Evelyn answered. "But it doesn't stop me wishing I had her in my arms right now. We waited so long for a baby that now we have our beloved Isabelle, I hate to leave her for even a minute."

Tommy put his arm around Evelyn and pulled her closer to his side. "How on earth shall you manage when she starts school?"

"That's years away." Evelyn rested her head on Tommy's shoulder. "Perhaps I will have learned to accept necessary absences by then."

"Perhaps," he echoed with a doubtful note in his voice.

"We are agreed that she shouldn't be a boarder?" Evelyn asked anxiously.

Tommy squeezed his wife's shoulder. "You have asked me that same question at least a hundred times. Each time you have asked it, I have told you that if you would prefer Isabelle to be driven to school, and returned home to us at the end of the school day, then that is what we shall do."

She sighed. "Yes, you have reassured me constantly. Thank you. I know it's not usual for children in the Christie family to be day students."

"I don't think I could bear for her to be a boarder either," Tommy admitted, and gave a small shudder. "Imagine not being able to visit her in the nursery to say goodnight before dinner."

That would be terrible. However, for Evelyn, she couldn't bear to think of waking up each morning and not hurrying to the nursery to see Isabelle's sweet face lighting up in a gummy grin.

Evelyn had spent years raising her beloved Gordon Setter dogs, Nancy, Davey, and Mary, and loved them to distraction. She thought she was prepared for the love she would feel for her child, but she hadn't expected the all-consuming emotion she felt as soon as she realised she was pregnant. Which, of course, was nothing compared to the feeling she experienced when the doctor placed Isabelle in her arms for the first time.

Isabelle, it turned out, had been in rather a hurry to arrive and was born a few weeks early during their summer stay in Scarborough. Their dear friend, and village doctor, Teddy Mainwaring, delivered her at the Majestic Hotel, where family and friends were staying for an extended break.

"Did I tell you that it is my belief that Elijah will be a big brother by next summer?" Evelyn asked, hoping a little idle chitchat would take her mind off how far away she was from her beloved daughter.

"Really?" Tommy squeezed Evelyn's hand. "That is marvellous news. Teddy and Isolde must be thrilled."

"Now you're not to say anything, Tommy. I don't think Teddy knows yet."

"Then perhaps, my dear," Tommy said in a gently chiding voice, "you shouldn't be saying anything until Isolde is ready to announce her news."

"I'm not betraying a confidence," Evelyn replied. "It's just a feeling I have. Something about the way she looks. It's quite possible Isolde doesn't even know herself yet."

"How can that be?"

Evelyn rested her head on Tommy's shoulder. "It's a female thing. Apparently, Mrs O'Connell knew I was expecting Isabelle before we even travelled to Derbyshire."

"Goodness. How intriguing. Yet you yourself did not know?"

"I did not," she confirmed. "I didn't suspect until after you had left."

"I still think—"

"Yes," Evelyn cut in. "I know. You still think I should have told you by letter."

"No," he retorted. "I think you should have come home immediately, and told me personally."

"You know why I didn't do that. I promised to help Hugh with the dogs. I was not about to leave halfway through their training and break my promise, and I did tell you to your face rather than impersonally by letter." Evelyn lifted her head and looked out of the window. "Now, why don't you tell me about your old friend? The one who is a master at Docere House."

"Ralph Gower," Tommy said. "A thoroughly decent chap."

"That doesn't tell me very much."

"Well, now, let me see." Tommy tilted his head. "I'm not exactly sure how much I can tell you about Ralph. We trained at the same time, but after serving together for a few months, he was transferred."

"Transferred where?" Evelyn had no trouble picking up on the reluctant note in Tommy's voice. They had been married long enough for her to know when he was hiding something from her. "Do tell the whole story, Tommy."

"I'm afraid I can't," he replied. "Not even if I wanted to. But I'm afraid I know little more than Ralph was sent to work in intelligence."

Evelyn gasped. "How exciting! The Secret Service, or MI1. Do you think he will tell us?"

"No," Tommy said tersely. "And you must not ask him. One doesn't know who is listening, and Ralph's work in intelligence shouldn't be made common knowledge."

"But surely now the war is over, it's—"

He held up a hand. "No more, Evelyn. You were about to say it's safe now. One simply cannot trust that things in Europe will stay calm. The last war may be over, and I pray there will never be another. However, the secret work that brave soldiers such as Ralph Gower undertook should never be spoken about."

Evelyn lay her head back on Tommy's shoulder and tightened her grip on his hand. The only person he ever really discussed the war with was their village vicar, John Capes. The subject of the war was the only one that caused Tommy's usually open and affable countenance to change to one of guarded coldness.

Tommy disliked not sharing everything with his wife. Yet no matter how many times she asked, or even spoke casually about the war, he felt defensive. His experiences during the war were not something he wanted to bring into his marriage. The hardship, the loss, and the brutality of war were not fit discussion topics between a man and his wife. His opinion of that would never change, despite his knowledge that Evelyn would be a sympathetic audience.

"Here we are now, my lord," Albert announced from the front seat, with no sign that he had heard even a single word of their conversation.

The car made a right turn from the country road onto a private lane. Evelyn craned her neck. "I don't see it."

Tommy smiled indulgently. "You won't see the main building for another couple of minutes. The drive is long and rather winding."

"I can hear happiness in your voice," Evelyn said as she looked round at him.

To his surprise, Tommy found that he was indeed smiling. "I have fond memories of my time at Docere House."

Evelyn wrinkled her nose. "Even though you were a boarder?"

"You talk about boarding as if it was an archaic punishment. I enjoyed boarding with my chums."

"But—"

"No, dear," Tommy said with exaggerated patience. "That isn't what either of us wants for Isabelle. If she were to choose to board herself, perhaps when she was in the senior school, I would support that decision."

"I'm sure she won't," Evelyn said with a note of desperation in her voice. "I'm certain she will wish to stay home at Hessleham Hall with us."

Now was not the time to press the matter with Evelyn. Isabelle was barely two months old. It was quite right that Evelyn could only imagine Isabelle relying on her family and nanny. He could scarcely comprehend that one day she would be eleven years old, ready for senior school, and no doubt have a mind of her own. If the women of his family were anything to go by, she would be a headstrong and independent young lady. He only hoped he could live up to the role as the father of such a girl.

"There now," he said. "If you look through the trees on the left, you will get your first glimpse of Docere House."

Evelyn did as he suggested, then turned to him in delight. "It looks jolly nice."

"I did tell you it was," he said. "I know you were expecting some sort of Victorian workhouse, but it isn't at all like that."

"No," she replied, sounding somewhat mollified. "I see that now."

"Wait until you see inside," he said. "I think you'll be surprised."

Presently, the car stopped in a huge circular driveway. "I feel rather excited."

"I am glad." Tommy smiled at his wife. "It is much easier for everyone if you are happy about Isabelle's education."

Evelyn worried her bottom lip. "Perhaps a governess would be best. Maybe—"

"We've discussed this matter until we are both blue in the face," he said gently. "We agreed that a school where Isabelle can mix with other children would be best."

"Are we certain she shouldn't go to the village school with Josephine and her cousins?"

Evelyn's dearest friend, Isolde Mainwaring, had taught at the village school until she married the doctor, and had spoken many times about how well equipped it was—especially for a small village. While he had no reason to think standards had slipped since Isolde had left, he believed a private education was the correct choice for his child. Evelyn's sister, Millicent Wilder, sent her children to the village school, but that was understandable. He didn't think her husband Reg's hospital doctor's salary would cover private school tuition for their six children.

"Yes, we are," he said firmly. "Whether we like it or not, or even agree with it or not, Isabelle has been born into a particular station in life. You can't think that attending Docere House harmed Harry, Constance, Grace, or me."

"No, of course not." Evelyn looked at him with a worried expression. "Though it did little good for Eddie."

"Eddie was rotten before he ever attended school. As the only boy after six girls, he was thoroughly spoiled."

"I always felt sorry for him because his mother died when he was so young," Evelyn said. "But Aunt Em says he took after his father and wasn't at all like his mother."

"I'm sure that's right." Albert had turned off the engine and walked round to open the car door for Evelyn. "Now come along. Miss Davenport will be expecting us."

As Evelyn exited the vehicle, Tommy wondered what it would be like to meet with Miss Davenport again. The last time they had seen her was when Eddie's father, Charles, and then Eddie himself, had been killed at Hessleham Hall. Had it not been for the deaths of his cousin and uncle, Tommy would never have inherited his title. Sometimes he wished he had not, yet equally there were occasions when he was grateful he was Lord Northmoor. Having a title definitely had advantages when there was something one wanted doing quickly.

Tommy opened his own car door and joined

Evelyn, who was looking up at the grand old building in awe. "It looks just like a house."

"A very large house," Tommy said with a chuckle. "Thank you, Albert. We will be about an hour, I should think."

Albert inclined his head. "Very good, my lord."

Tommy strode up the stairs and pressed the little button placed discretely to the side of the door. Within moments, the door swung open to reveal a young woman in a neat grey uniform.

"Lord and Lady Northmoor to see Miss Davenport," he announced. "We have an appointment at ten."

"Of course." She bobbed her knee deferentially. "Please follow me."

"She looks just like a housemaid," Evelyn whispered.

"That's because that's exactly what she is," he replied.

"But this is a school."

"It is," Tommy agreed. "But it's also a house full of people who all need taking care of."

"Was this once Miss Davenport's home?" Evelyn asked. "Before it was a school, I mean?"

"I hadn't ever thought of that." Tommy frowned. "Though it would make perfect sense, wouldn't it?"

"Yes, it would." Evelyn's lips thinned.

On the previous occasion they had met Julia Davenport, it became known that Julia's father,

Herbert, had lost Docere House in a bet with Tommy's Uncle Charles. Julia had been suspected of killing Charles, so desperately had she wanted the school back in her family's ownership. It made more sense that the school had, in fact, once been their family home rather than simply a school building.

Evelyn could see why anyone would be infuriated about losing such a lovely place. The red brick façade gave the building a homely look while the many Georgian-style windows gave the inside of the school a light and airy feel. She had grown to love Hessleham Hall, but it was a purely functional building compared to Docere House, which was both pretty as well as impressive.

The maid led them down a bright corridor, then through a door into a large room with several chairs and an enormous desk. A robust-looking woman with steel-grey hair continued typing ferociously on an impressive black typewriter even as she looked up to observe their arrival.

"Lord and Lady Northmoor, I presume?"

"Yes, that's right." Tommy turned to look at Evelyn. Her look of wonder no doubt matched his own. Although the woman looked up with a polite expression, she had not stopped her work.

"Do take a seat and I shall let Miss Davenport know you are here." The imposing secretary flipped a page on her notebook with one hand and lifted the receiver of the telephone with the other. "Lord and

Lady Northmoor are here. Yes, of course. Daisy, a tea tray, if you please."

The maid bobbed her knee once more and rushed from the room. At the same time, the door opposite opened and Julia Davenport came out to meet them. "Lord and Lady Northmoor. How wonderful it is to see you both once more. And, if I may say, in much happier circumstances."

Tommy shook Miss Davenport's proffered hand. "Yes, indeed."

"Tea will be along presently, Miss Davenport." The secretary looked up and gave a quick smile while her fingers danced across the keys of the typewriter.

"Thank you, Nanny."

Tommy couldn't help but ask. "Nanny?"

"Please take a seat." Julia Davenport indicated the chairs across from the black leather chair that was clearly her own. While the secretary's desk was orderly—papers in neat piles, folders in precise stacks, and the typewriter itself placed at an exact angle—the head teacher's desk was a maelstrom of chaos. "Miss Bunting was my nanny. We kept her on even after there were no longer any children in the family. Jolly good decision, as it turns out, as she's an extremely efficient secretary."

"That's good to hear," Evelyn said. "You will be pleased to hear Lord Northmoor has fond memories of his time at Docere House."

"I'm extremely pleased to hear it," said Julia Davenport, shuffling through the papers on her desk. "I was surprised to receive your application for a place here for your daughter."

Evelyn cast a worried look at Tommy. "Were you?"

"Why yes, Lord Northmoor." The head teacher smiled. "If it hadn't been for your kind intervention after the death of your uncle, goodness only knows what would have become of Docere House."

Tommy waved a hand. "I simply put right a dreadful wrong."

"That may be how you see it, but it isn't at all how I see it," Julia replied. "Owning the school again meant we no longer had to send exorbitant sums of money to your uncle every quarter. The school has prospered now that we can spend fees on children and their education. Which, of course, is the most important thing about a school—the children."

"How is your father?" Evelyn asked.

"Oh, father is very well, thank you." Julia's handsome face lit up as she smiled. "I believe he is teaching chemistry this morning. Of course, he retired years ago, but if there is ever a need for an extra teacher, he is excited to be asked to help. There isn't a thing he wouldn't do for the school."

"I wanted to ask after one of your chemistry masters, actually," Tommy said. "An old army friend of mine. We keep in touch. Infrequent letters, you know, but I am certain he is still employed here. Ralph Gower."

"Oh." Julia looked down at her untidy desk. "Oh, I see. How unfortunate."

"Unfortunate?" Tommy echoed.

"He's been taken ill this morning. My father is teaching in his place."

Tommy got to his feet. "Is there anything I can do for him?"

Evelyn reached up a hand and rested it on his elbow. "Sit down, darling. I'm sure Miss Davenport has everything under control."

"Indeed," the teacher said soothingly. "The doctor has been out to see Mr Gower. A minor gastrointestinal issue, apparently. Rather ghastly for poor Mr Gower, but no cause for alarm. At the moment, his physical illness is the least of my concerns."

"How so?" Tommy asked sharply, his hackles rising at the thought of any slight against his old friend.

"I'm afraid Mr Gower has been exhibiting some rather odd behaviour."

"Odd?" Tommy raised an eyebrow. "What, exactly, does that mean?"

"He hasn't been himself." Julia drew in a deep breath. "Several members of staff have seen him muttering to himself in the corridors. He frequently looks behind him as though he believes he's being followed. And he's spent an inordinate amount of time in his laboratory on some new invention that he flatly refuses to share any information about—either with his assistant or anyone else."

"I assume that means you, too?"

"Yes," she said sadly. "While I am more than happy for Mr Gower, or any other member of staff, to use school equipment after hours, I would expect them to share their work with their peers. Mr Gower has been exceedingly secretive and I'm afraid it seems he is on the verge of a breakdown."

"How sad," murmured Evelyn.

"Doesn't sound like Gower at all." Tommy shook his head.

"At the risk of sounding impertinent, Lord Northmoor, I understand this sort of thing happens to many soldiers after they return from war. Perhaps your friend has buckled under the strain of the atrocities he witnessed."

Tommy opened his mouth to speak, then closed it again. He didn't know what Ralph Gower had, or hadn't, seen during the war as he spent much of it working in a different regiment to Tommy doing goodness knew what. He could have been sitting behind a desk as he worked on breaking codes, or some other desk-bound work, but equally he could have been based out in the field gathering intelligence from behind enemy lines.

"I would like to see him, please."

"Of course, Lord Northmoor." Julia Davenport got to her feet just as a tap sounded from the other side of the door. "That will be tea. Perhaps we should complete the application for Lady Isabelle first?"

The hairs on the back of Tommy's neck stood on end, and he suppressed a shudder. "I'd rather not, if that's all the same to you."

"You don't want Lady Isabelle's name on the waiting list at Docere House?" the head teacher frowned.

"Darling?" Evelyn had also got to her feet, and she rested a hand on his elbow. "Have you changed your mind?"

"Not at all." He tried to smile, but he was aware his face formed a grimace rather than an expression of pleasure. "I feel...oh it's so hard to put into words what I feel. I have an intense impression that something is dreadfully wrong. I simply must see Captain Gower immediately."

The door opened, and Daisy, the housemaid, entered laden with a tea tray. "Tea, Miss Davenport."

"Yes," Julia agreed distractedly. "Put it over there."

Daisy followed the direction of Julia's hand gesture and placed the tray on a low table near the window. "Can I get anything else for you?"

Julia's large brown eyes stared at the maid in

confusion for a moment before she blinked, then nodded. "Yes, thank you. I must see Miss Cambridge and Mr Adams immediately."

The maid showed no signs of noticing that anything was wrong as she hurried from the room.

"Who are those people?"

"Miss Cambridge is my assistant. Mr Adams is a junior colleague who works with Mr Gower. Father didn't think he was quite ready for teaching the lower sixth just yet, which is why he is doing it himself. They can be quite unruly. Boys, you know." She looked down at the sheet of paper she had put uppermost on her desk earlier. "Mr Adams will take you to see Mr Gower and then Miss Cambridge will show you around the school. She was a pupil here herself, so ask her anything and she will be only too pleased to give you an honest answer. Then perhaps you will return to my office and we will process the application for Lady Isabelle. Though, of course, as I said earlier, there was really no need for you to make an application."

"Why?" Tommy snapped, his agitation rising.

"I would have been quite happy to—"

"No." He held up a hand to stop the head teacher's words. "Lady Northmoor and I don't want the sort of favours my Uncle Charles insisted on. We don't wish to pay money to secure our daughter's place at Docere House."

"A couple of years ago you performed a great

kindness for my father and I, Lord Northmoor," Julia said quietly. "We would therefore welcome any child of yours at this school without payment. I'm only sorry that I didn't find a graceful way to communicate that to you before now. It would have saved you an unnecessary journey."

A tap sounded on the door once more. This time when it opened, a young woman stood there in a neat navy skirt and jacket. She wore dark sensible shoes and had an air of composure about her, not unlike that of Miss Bunting.

"Ah, Miss Cambridge." Julia peered behind the woman. "Where is Mr Adams?"

"I'm not sure, Miss Davenport." Miss Cambridge smiled reassuringly. "I imagine I shall find him over in the science wing. Either there or in the masters' quarters. At any rate, Lord and Lady Northmoor, how pleased I am to meet you both."

Tommy's tension diminished somewhat at the assistant's calming presence. "How do you do?"

"Very well, thank you." The assistant turned to her superior. "What was it you wanted me, and Mr Adams, to do for you, Miss Davenport?"

Miss Cambridge was a tall, blonde woman who appeared to be in her early twenties. She was very attractive, despite her almost rigid stance and very proper demeanour. As the head teacher had said her assistant had been a pupil at Docere House herself, it was probable Miss Cambridge attended at the same time as Tommy's sisters.

"Lord Northmoor wishes to see his old friend, Mr Gower."

"Oh, I'm not certain he's—" Miss Cambridge's expression turned reluctant and a worried frown puckered her brow.

"Now, please."

A faint blush stained the assistant's cheeks as she nodded her acquiescence. "Of course, Miss Davenport."

She then stood back and indicated that Tommy and Evelyn should exit the room before her. Tommy wanted to grab hold of the woman's shoulders and shake her. For some reason, he couldn't escape the feeling that time was of the essence and every moment they spent being exceedingly pleasant to each other was time wasted.

~

Evelyn wished they had never left the house that morning. If only she had sent a carefully worded letter to Julia Davenport, asking for Isabelle's name to be placed on the school's waiting list, but asking if they could be excused from the obligatory meeting with the headmistress and school tour given they had already met Julia and Tommy, and his siblings had attended

Docere House. Ordinarily, she abhorred preferential treatment given to them because of Tommy's title, but on this occasion she wished she'd asked for it.

"The science wing is in Elm House," Miss Cambridge said brightly, as though she was completely unaware there was anything wrong. "Over on our left is Birch House. We teach English and mathematics in that building."

"Are all the buildings named after trees?" Evelyn asked. The answer was obvious, but she wanted to say something to try to break the uncomfortable atmosphere. After all, Miss Cambridge was trying so hard.

"Yes, that's correct, Lady Northmoor." The head's assistant smiled. "It makes it easier for the children to identify the buildings. If you look at the nameplate near the door of Birch House as we pass by, you can see both the name printed and a picture of a birch tree."

"Oh, yes, I see that." Evelyn nodded.

"We could have gone through the main building and out through one of the rear doors to reach Elm House, but I thought you would prefer to walk outside. It's such an unseasonably warm day." She didn't look at Tommy, but focussed her attention on Evelyn. Which was probably wise, given Tommy's face was a mask of barely repressed frustration.

"We are indeed being lucky with the weather," Evelyn responded politely, while wishing she could think of something witty or intelligent to say that would liven up their boring conversation.

"Are we nearly there?" Tommy demanded.

Miss Cambridge shot him a concerned glance before she nodded enthusiastically. "We are. Elm House is the next building along. The schoolrooms are on the ground floor and the masters' rooms are on the upper floor. Ah, good. Look, here is Mr Adams."

"Captain Gower's assistant?" Tommy asked in a clipped tone.

It hadn't escaped Evelyn's notice that Tommy had started referring to his old friend using his army rank as soon as he had been told his friend was unwell. His agitated state both puzzled and concerned her. It wasn't like Tommy to overreact. As far as she knew, he hadn't stayed in close touch with Mr Gower, so, to her at least, it was plausible the war had unbalanced the poor man's mind—even after nearly five years.

"Miss Cambridge?" Mr Adams walked over to them.

"This is Lord and Lady Northmoor." The assistant stood back as she made the introductions. "Lord and Lady Northmoor, this is Mr Bertie Adams, Ralph Gower's assistant."

"I understand Captain Gower is unwell?"

"I'm afraid so, Lord Northmoor. We telephoned

for the doctor earlier this morning, and he left medicine, but Mr Gower has not yet picked up."

"His illness is now physical? The mental instabilities he was experiencing have not continued?" Tommy rapped out the questions.

"You are correct," Mr Adams said.

"I must see him," Tommy said desperately.

"He may not wish to have visitors," the other man said nervously. "The nausea, you know, it left him—"

"He will see me," Tommy said confidently. "I insist you take me to his room immediately."

"Very well, Lord Northmoor." Mr Adams exchanged a look with Miss Cambridge that Evelyn interpreted as anxiety mixed with resignation.

Mr Adams led the way into Elm House, with Tommy following closely behind. Evelyn walked alongside Miss Cambridge.

"Perhaps I should go back to the main house now."

"Please don't," Evelyn implored. "I should hate to be left alone while the two men visit Mr Gower."

"Oh, of course, Lady Northmoor." She smiled and Evelyn thought, not for the first time, that the head's assistant was a very beautiful woman. "I wasn't thinking."

Evelyn was perfectly content to stand in a corridor and wait for her husband to visit his old army friend, but she thought she might find out more information about Ralph's state of mind from the other woman.

They walked to the end of the corridor and then up a flight of wide stairs. At the second door along, Mr Adams knocked smartly. There was no answer that Evelyn could hear from her position standing against the windowsill.

"Let me," Tommy urged. He stepped forward and twisted the doorknob, calling out as he opened the door. "Captain Gower? Hello! It's Major Christie. I hope you don't mind, but I'm coming in."

Mr Adams looked over his shoulder at Miss Cambridge. "This is all extremely extraordinary behaviour. I should hope I won't get into trouble."

"Don't be absurd," Evelyn retorted. "Lord Northmoor has taken it upon himself to enter Mr Gower's private quarters. You can be assured that any repercussions there may be will be accepted by him."

"Evelyn!" Tommy's voice sounded clear from inside the room. "I need you in here immediately."

The two staff members shared yet another worried look, but Evelyn paid them no mind as she hurried to join her husband.

"Tommy, what is it?" Evelyn called out as she entered a small but comfortable-looking living room.

"Come through to the bedroom," he urged.

Evelyn hurried to do as he asked. "Oh, Tommy. I'm so very sorry."

Ralph Gower was slumped sideways in his bed. A book and a sheet of paper lay on top of the bedspread. A large blue stain suggested an uncapped pen had been dropped onto the cover. To the side of the ink stain was an open Bible. On the nightstand was a letter which was addressed to Ralph.

Although his eyes were open, it was quite clear that the poor man would see nothing on earth ever again. Ralph Gower was quite dead.

2

"How could this happen?" Tommy paced the small room knowing his recent behaviour had seemed out of proportion to the school staff, but not able to explain his deep-seated belief that something was horribly wrong. Now his fears had been proven correct, his mood had swung from irrational concern to anger.

"One can never be sure with gastrointestinal illnesses," Bertie said in a nervous tone. "Sometimes they do turn deadly in a short space of time. Lady Northmoor, perhaps you'd like to step outside? This must be very distressing for you."

"No thank you," Evelyn replied curtly.

"What time was the doctor here?" Tommy tried to remember he was in a civilian situation but failed —his words sounded more like a military command than a question.

"About two hours ago," Miss Cambridge's voice sounded from Mr Gower's sitting room. He was glad she hadn't come any closer. Bertie Adams was right —this was no sight for a lady. Evelyn excluded, of course. After all, this was hardly the first dead body she had seen.

"And he left medicine?"

"It's here on the dressing table." Bertie picked up the bottle and turned it around to read the label. "It's more a tonic, really. To help replace lost fluids and prevent dehydration."

Tommy leaned over Ralph and pinched the skin on the back of his hand then let go. Ralph's skin bounced back into shape immediately. "Dehydration doesn't seem to have been an issue."

"How long had he been ill?" Evelyn asked the science master's assistant. Without waiting for an answer, she turned to the open door and spoke to Miss Cambridge. "Please go back to the main house and call for the police. Let them know there has been a suspicious death."

"Suspicious?" Bertie repeated.

"Ordinarily healthy people do not tend to die from gastroenteritis," Tommy said. "If, indeed, that is what ailed Ralph."

"Don't you believe the doctor?"

"Has Miss Cambridge left?" Tommy looked to Evelyn who nodded in response. He then looked back at Bertie Adams who was sweating profusely despite the coolness of the room. "Now please answer my wife's question: for how long had Captain Gower been ill?"

Bertie glanced at the dead body of his mentor, then ran a finger along the collar of his starched white shirt and pulled at his navy tie. "He had been unwell for some time."

"With stomach flu?"

"That particular illness is more recent."

"Explain what you mean," Tommy ordered.

"What Lord Northmoor requires from you," Evelyn said in a gentle voice, "is a complete history of the changes in Mr Gower's behaviour and health. Please do not give us what you believe may have been going on, but just the facts."

Bertie Adams nodded gratefully at Evelyn and then turned to address Tommy. "Mr Gower was perfectly fine at the start of the term in September. It was perhaps a couple of weeks after the term started that his behaviour changed. On several occasions, I saw him mumbling to himself as he was walking along. Other staff noticed that he seemed jumpy and would sometimes turn quickly, as though he thought someone was following him. His concentration was completely shot to pieces."

"It seemed, perhaps, that there was a great weight on Mr Gower's mind?" Evelyn suggested.

"Yes," he answered enthusiastically. "That's exactly it. It was like he was so preoccupied with something, he couldn't focus on even the simplest of tasks. I had to step in and teach classes in his place a couple of times. Then this last week, things escalated. Poor Mr Gower was physically trembling. He complained of headaches and seemed dizzy and disorientated. Yesterday he complained of a stomach upset and then this morning he was too ill to teach, and so we telephoned for the doctor."

"Whose decision was that?"

Bertie blinked at Tommy's question. "I kept Miss Davenport apprised of Mr Gower's condition and this morning she asked Nanny Bunting to make the telephone call."

"Do you mean you reported to the head that Mr Gower was mumbling to himself and having difficulty concentrating?" Although Tommy made a real attempt to keep his voice calm, he himself could hear the accusatory tone coming through loud and clear.

"Well yes, Lord Northmoor." Bertie squirmed. "I know it seems like tittle-tattling, but his behaviour was affecting his work, and I thought the headmistress needed to know."

More likely the man thought the headmistress might discipline Ralph, and there he was, Bertie Adams, ready and waiting to step into the other man's teaching shoes. Although Julia, and certainly her father, seemed to believe Mr Adams was not yet ready for the more senior position.

"All right. Thank you for your help. You can leave us now."

"Yes, Lord Northmoor. Thank you, Lord Northmoor."

As soon as the outer door closed behind the assistant, Tommy expressed a frustration sigh.

"You were jolly brusque."

"The man is a bumbling fool." Tommy strode over to the window. "I find it so difficult to believe a grown man is happy to go telling tales to teacher."

"If Ralph's behaviour was affecting his work, and Mr Adams had already discussed the matter with him, I don't see that he had any choice."

"Hmph." Tommy grunted. "Ralph isn't at all like he described."

Evelyn walked over to him and placed a hand on his arm. "Do stop stalking about, darling. While I understand how upset you are, you must realise that the Ralph you knew during the war years isn't necessarily the man he has been recently."

"He's a very composed man, precise in everything he does. Absolutely nothing ruffles him. A man cannot change the very essence of his personality despite the passing of time." He gazed into the face of his wife and wished that she could have known Ralph as he did. Then she would understand that while her words were reasonable, they were not correct.

"Should we look at the whatever it was he was

writing?" Evelyn edged nearer the bed. "Especially if the police are on their way. Otherwise I don't think we will get the chance after they arrive."

"Whatever happened to us not sleuthing anymore after Isabelle was born?" Tommy couldn't help but tease Evelyn.

"That was before a dear friend of yours was killed practically under our very noses," she retorted as she leaned over Ralph and twisted her head at an angle to look at the writing paper.

If Ralph had indeed been a 'dear friend', Tommy would've kept in better contact with him instead of a single rushed letter at Christmastime. However, he was glad Evelyn had answered his unspoken question about whether or not they should investigate Ralph's death. He was a comrade, one of the few people who had known Tommy during the most difficult time of his life. Ralph Gower deserved justice.

"What does it say?"

"It begins 'My dear Tommy'." Evelyn glanced at him.

"It's for me?"

"I'm sure there are lots of people named Tommy, but I can't imagine that there was more than one coming to Docere House today. The letter goes onto say, *'It may seem strange me writing to you when you are coming here today, but in the event I am not well enough to meet with you, I need you to know—'*"

"Yes?" Tommy waved his hand, indicating that Evelyn should hurry reading the rest of the letter. "What else does it say?"

"Nothing." Evelyn stood upright once more and moved as far away from the body as she could without leaving the room. "You can see where he dropped his pen on the bedsheet. There's also a corresponding squiggle on the paper which suggests Ralph passed out in the middle of writing to you."

"What an inconvenient moment for unconsciousness to take him." Tommy pulled a hand through his hair in pure agitation. "I don't mean that as harshly as it sounds. Of course I don't."

"We shall work it out," Evelyn said soothingly. "He was leaning on a book to write the letter. I can't see what that book is. The other is a King James Bible."

"I don't remember Ralph being particularly religious."

"You weren't either. People do change, darling."

"Yes." Tommy stopped pacing and looked down at the carpet. "Yes, I suppose they do. If you agree that we must find out what happened to Ralph, then we need to tell Albert we shall not be needing the car again for some considerable time."

"I will go let him know he should go back to Hessleham Hall and we shall telephone for him to return when we are ready. He can let Nora know we will be gone longer than expected."

"Thank you," Tommy said. "I know you'd really rather go home to Isabelle."

"Isabelle will be happier with two content parents. Right now, Tommy, you are extremely dissatisfied with this situation and I can see why." Evelyn cupped Tommy's cheek with her hand. "Until we find out what happened to Ralph, we shall stay here at Docere House."

Evelyn left Tommy, who had recommenced his customary pacing, and hurried to the front of the main building to find Albert.

"Ah, Lady Northmoor," he said as Evelyn approached. "I have something I wish to discuss with Lord Northmoor before we leave."

"We won't be leaving for some time, I'm afraid, Albert. Can I help?"

"I'm sure you can, my lady." Albert grinned. "Follow me to the stables."

She really shouldn't waste time looking at the Docere House horses, but Evelyn found herself following the young chauffeur anyway. A few minutes away from the awful scene of Ralph's death wouldn't hurt. She took several deep breaths to clear the terrible stench of death from her nostrils and hurried along behind Albert.

"What do you want to show me?" Evelyn asked as Albert stopped, facing one of the many stalls.

"Look in there, my lady."

Albert stood back to allow Evelyn to approach the stall. To her surprise, it did not contain a horse. "Albert?"

"Look closer, my lady."

Evelyn did as he suggested, and finally, in one of the dimly lit corners, she saw a couple of kittens sleeping on an old horse blanket. "You brought me here to see kittens, Albert?"

He looked disconcerted at her quizzically raised brow. "We could really do with a good mouser in our stables, my lady."

"That's what you wished to discuss with Lord Northmoor?"

"Indeed." Albert took his cap from his head and twisted it nervously in his fingers. "Lord Northmoor said if we heard of any available kittens, we should bring them home."

"Don't we already have cats in the stables?" She tried to remember the last time she had been to that part of the estate, but she could not. It had been months since she had been riding. Pregnancy and motherhood were not conducive to such a pastime.

"I'm afraid not. One cat died, the vet said from old age. Then the other one ran away. Perhaps he didn't enjoy being alone, or maybe he thought the grass was greener somewhere else."

"They do look rather sweet." Despite knowing she had other, better, things with which she should occupy her mind, Evelyn opened the catch on the stall and walked in.

"Do be careful, my lady," Albert called. "Perhaps you should let me go into the stable and bring the kittens out to you."

Evelyn didn't care if her outfit got dirty, or if she smelled of horses. It was worth it to spend a few quick moments with the kittens after the horror of what she had just witnessed. Especially, as Albert said, getting kittens for the estate stables would help Tommy.

They looked up as they heard her moving across the straw towards them. She counted four kittens, more than she had originally thought. Evelyn sat next to them and allowed them to crawl onto her lap so she could have a good look at them. "We shall take the ginger one, for I know that is a boy. I also rather like this one."

Evelyn held up one kitten for Albert to see. "The black one with a white patch over his eye. Good choice, my lady. Should I ask if those two kittens are available? They look old enough to leave their mother."

She stood, shook out her skirt, then walked back to Albert. "Yes please, Albert. Then you should head back to Hessleham Hall. Lord Northmoor will telephone when we are ready for you to drive back and collect us."

Albert put his cap back on his head. "Of course, my lady. I will see to that immediately."

He rushed off to do her bidding, and she marvelled at how unconcerned he seemed to be that she and Tommy were staying at Docere House longer than planned. She would have been positively bouncing with curiosity to find out the reason their departure was delayed, but Albert hadn't asked a single question. Of course, it wasn't his place to question directions he was given, but he hadn't looked either surprised or in the least bit inquisitive about her instructions.

Perhaps only a certain number of people were naturally inquisitorial by nature, and it just so happened that she and Tommy were two of those people. She couldn't imagine not looking into any of the mysteries they had faced over the last few years, though she supposed others would either look the other way or actively run away from such problems.

She looked back toward Elm House. She'd given Tommy enough time by himself. Now they must work side by side to discover what on earth had happened to Ralph Gower.

"Evelyn, you've been gone for simply ages." Tommy struggled to keep the note of frustration from his voice. Didn't she realise how important it was that they discovered what had caused Ralph's death?

"Sorry, darling, Albert wanted to show me some kittens."

"Kittens?" Tommy shook his head in confusion. "Never mind. I don't want to know. Tell me later. You must see what I have discovered."

"Have you found a clue?"

"I certainly have." Tommy indicated the Bible, then leaned over and lifted the book into his hands. "Judges 14:12 *'And Samson said unto them, I will now put forth a riddle unto you: if ye can certainly declare it me within the seven days of the feast, and find it out, then I will give you thirty sheets and thirty changes of garments:'*"

"I don't understand."

"You'll never guess which word he underlined."

She thought for a moment. "I think I will. Riddle. It's riddle, isn't it?"

He should have known his wife and her sharp mind would rise to the challenge. "What do you think it means?"

"What we know so far," Evelyn said. "Is that Ralph knew you were coming to Docere House and had begun to write a letter to you saying there was something he needed to tell you. He left his Bible open with the one word underlined 'riddle'. I think that means he has left you a riddle to solve."

"About what?" Tommy carefully replaced the Bible on the bed.

"He was unwell. His letter specifically refers to that fact."

"Do you think it is possible he knew he was dying?" Tommy hated to think of his old comrade in bed, knowing he was desperately ill, and deciding to write him a letter. "He knew I was coming, so that part makes sense, even though we haven't corresponded regularly since the war ended. But what could he want me to know?"

"Who killed him?" Evelyn suggested.

"You think he was murdered?" Tommy kept his voice low, even though there was no one to hear him.

"Don't you?" She held up a hand and counted off the other things that they knew. "He was acting strangely, his behaviour was markedly different to normal, he thought he was being followed, his illness progressed rapidly from what the doctor believed was a simple case of gastroenteritis to death."

"That suggests poison."

"Poison and the prior knowledge that someone wanted him dead, perhaps."

"Are we jumping to conclusions?" Tommy wondered.

"Maybe we are. But if that is the case, why would he leave you a riddle? Why not just say what he wanted to? He's leaving us breadcrumbs to follow."

There was logic in Evelyn's suggestion, but he still thought it was a stretch. "Let's say this is a murder. What's to say the murderer didn't discover the letter, and the Bible clue, and get rid of them so they wouldn't be found? Ralph couldn't possibly have known we would discover his body."

"A Bible on the bed of a dying man and a half-written letter to his old friend. Why would anyone other than us think that was something worth investigating? Even allowing for the fact the murderer was aware Ralph was dead before we visited him—why would they remove either item?"

"Let us follow your train of thought through for a moment," Tommy agreed. "We need a riddle to solve. Where might a man who knew he was dying leave a riddle?"

"The letter and the Bible are in open view. Perhaps there is another clue that we have overlooked."

"Wouldn't he hide an important clue, especially if it is linked to his death?"

"Of course he would." Evelyn scanned the room impatiently. "He wouldn't want the murderer to find the clue that pointed to the fact his death was murder and possibly that person's identity."

"So you think that is hidden, but the riddle itself isn't? The information we need to solve the murder, if indeed that is what it is, is the answer to the riddle?"

"Precisely." Evelyn nodded, a grim look of determination on her face. "Look around, Tommy. You knew the man. You are more likely than I to see something that is ordinary and everyday, so does not stand out, but is perhaps out of place for a man like Ralph."

"All right," he agreed. "Let's start with what I know. Ralph was a military man, so keeps an orderly living space. We can see that is so. His sitting room and bedroom are immaculate. I know he worked in intelligence, so the setting of a riddle makes sense. He knew I was coming here today, and no doubt would know we have been involved in solving several crimes over the last few years."

"The newspaper articles are becoming rather tiresome," Evelyn commented. "The number of letters we receive asking us to investigate this and that, increases with each story printed about us. If it continues, I shall have to engage a secretary simply to deal with that correspondence alone."

"Why don't you just throw them on the fire?" Tommy asked as he moved into the sitting room to look around.

"I couldn't possibly do that," Evelyn said with a horrified expression. "People have taken the time and trouble to write to us. One day, there might be a real puzzle for us to solve instead of nonsense about missing cats, errant husbands, and ghosts in the night."

He thought it prudent not to say that, until today, Evelyn had sworn off solving mysteries. If that were so, why was she opening and reading the letters anxious strangers were sending? He made a mental note to ask her about that later.

"Come and look at this," he called. He pointed to the bookshelf nestled in a corner of the sitting room. "Does that look out of place to you?"

"Certainly it does," Evelyn agreed. "All the other books are neatly placed, whereas the spine of one book is sticking out slightly."

Tommy plucked the thin book from the bookshelf and turned it over in his hands. "*Poems* by Wilfred Owen."

"Open it," Evelyn urged.

Tommy did so, then looked up at Evelyn in excitement. "There are a series of numbers and letters written in pencil in the margins."

As he flicked through the pages, something fell out onto the bare boards of the living room floor. "What is it?"

"A copy of Ralph's war service record."

"Do you have yours?" She asked although she already knew the answer.

"Somewhere," he answered vaguely. "It's not

something I like to spend any time remembering, as you well know."

"Is there anything significant recorded?" She ignored his sour tone, which only made her wonder why he kept his own record, stored away with other mementoes such as letters she had written, in a battered suitcase atop of the wardrobe of his dressing room.

"Does this look like a different handwriting?" Tommy peered at the document, then held it out for Evelyn to see.

"It does," she said. "But wouldn't that be normal? I mean, surely the same person couldn't have been responsible for writing everything on a record card?"

"When we were discharged, we were given a copy of our record. The original would certainly have different handwriting, but you would think only one person copied the entries over onto the document we were given."

"*22nd February 1917 – Intelligence: Room 40.* What does that mean?"

"Room 40 was where code breakers originally worked. I think Ralph wrote that into his record himself to let me know that was his job when he moved into intelligence."

"Ralph was a code breaker?" Evelyn asked in awe. "Does that mean the numbers in the poetry book could be a code of some sort?"

Loud footsteps sounded in the corridor outside the sitting room and Tommy hurriedly put the war record back into the volume of poetry and stuffed the Wilfred Owen book into the inside pocket of his jacket.

"The police have arrived," Miss Carmichael announced unnecessarily as Detective Inspector Andrews and Detective Sergeant Montgomery entered the sitting room.

"I might have known you two would be here," the detective inspector said sardonically. "Has there ever been a dead body in the county of North Yorkshire without both of you in the vicinity?"

"We are here to register our daughter at the school as a pupil," Evelyn said with equal sarcasm.

The detective jerked his head towards Ralph's bedroom. "Is there a dead body in there?"

Much to his consternation, Tommy had to concede the detective's point. "Yes, there is."

"I rest my case." Shaking his head, he motioned to his detective sergeant to follow him. "Perhaps you and your lovely wife would be so good as to wait for us in the headmistress's office?"

The code in the poetry book:

R1:29,13

J3:12,9

I41:19, 11

3

Julia Davenport sat primly behind her desk, facing Tommy, Evelyn, and the two police detectives. Detective Inspector Andrews and Detective Sergeant Montgomery, who were based in York, had met Tommy and Evelyn on several previous occasions. While the junior detective seemed to accept their propensity to conduct their own investigations, the detective inspector was not so tolerant.

"Perhaps you can let my sergeant and I know what has happened here, Lord Northmoor?"

"You are in my office in my school, Detective Inspector." Miss Davenport leaned forward, placing her hands flat on the messy surface of her desk. "No disrespect to Lord and Lady Northmoor, but I think you should direct your enquiries to me. Surely I should hold seniority in my school?"

"Miss Davenport, have you seen the body of Mr Gower? Have you been in his room? Have you snooped through his personal possessions?" Detective Inspector Andrews eyed the school headmistress with what Evelyn, if pressed, could only describe as mild amusement in his gaze.

"Obviously, the answer to those questions is no," Julia Davenport snapped.

"As I thought." The detective turned to Tommy. "Lord Northmoor?"

"My wife and I are here to register our daughter's name at the school. Before our arrival, I knew that Mr Gower worked here as a teacher. I enquired after him when we arrived and was told by Mr Adams that he had been unwell recently. You should know that Mr Gower and I joined the army at almost the same time and trained alongside each other. I insisted that I be shown to his room as soon as I heard he was indisposed."

"Why?"

"That I can't explain," Tommy said. "All I can tell you is that I had a dreadful feeling something was horribly wrong."

Detective Inspector Andrews quirked his eyebrow in Tommy's direction. "I thought it was Lady Northmoor who generally had *feelings* about people or incidents."

"Is that a question?"

The detective's mouth tipped up at the corners. "If you like, yes."

"As you are well aware at this point in our acquaintance, my wife is well known for her intuition. On this occasion, I trusted my own, and was proven correct."

"May I ask," Evelyn said, "are we here because you intend to question us, or do I sense a thawing in the relationship between the North Yorkshire Police and the Christie family?"

"That is rather difficult to answer, Lady Northmoor. Let me just say that I have come to have a grudging admiration for the work that you have done in other cases. For some unfathomable reason, people seem to talk to you more than they do to the police. I don't like it, but I'm willing to work with it up to a certain point." He held up a hand. "That is clarified thus: if I find that you are not sharing things with me, or I believe that the nature of the investigation has become so dangerous that your lives may be in peril. If either of those points are reached, you must agree to step aside."

Evelyn folded her hands in her lap. "Despite your rather rude reference towards us snooping only a moment ago, I would say that what you suggest is most definitely a thawing."

"Do you agree with my stipulations?"

"I agree." Tommy looked at Evelyn.

"Yes," she replied with a concerted effort not to

look too smug about the fact that the police had finally recognised their efforts in the past.

"I assume the doctor was sent for when Mr Gower became ill?" Detective Inspector Andrews looked towards the headmistress.

Miss Davenport looked down at a piece of paper on her desk. "Yes. He came earlier today, and I believe left a tonic for Mr Gower, believing that his illness was no worse than uncomplicated gastroenteritis."

"Of course, a usually healthy person rarely dies from that particular illness," Evelyn said, looking at the detectives with meaning.

Detective Inspector Andrews shook his head. "Don't go thinking this is murder, Lady Northmoor. The poor man may just have had a weak constitution for all we know. Unless, of course, you know differently."

"You suspect that Mr Gower was murdered?" Julia Davenport gasped. "What grounds do you have? How can you make such an assumption? I hope you are not suggesting that one of my members of staff is, or could be, involved."

"You know how these things work, Miss Davenport," Tommy said apologetically, referring to the first case he and Evelyn had undertaken—which involved the untimely death of his uncle, the former Earl of Northmoor. "Unfortunately, everyone is a suspect until we know differently."

The headmistress pursed her lips. “I cannot allow my school to be turned into some macabre spectacle because you and Lady Northmoor wish to presume your old comrade’s death was murder. I have great sympathy for you. Mr Gower was an excellent teacher and a jolly good fellow. However, there’s no reason to believe this is anything other than the tragic loss of a man taken too soon by devastating illness.”

“My thoughts precisely, Miss Davenport.” Detective Inspector Andrews nodded his agreement wholeheartedly.

Evelyn glanced at Tommy. Now was perhaps a good time for them to mention the clues they had found in Ralph’s rooms. After all, they had taken the clues that they had found. It wasn’t being fair to the police that they had information and were not sharing it, particularly given the detectives’ very clear conditions for their involvement.

She would suggest to Tommy that they make a copy of the letters and numbers in the margin of the poem book and then put everything back where they had found it. If the police thereafter failed to find the clues, they could not be blamed for that. Technically, she knew that was breaking the Detective Inspector’s rule on sharing. However, she did not believe that it was hers or Tommy’s fault if the police were not as diligent, or capable, as them.

“We shall see what the doctor says when he

arrives," Tommy said. "But I think you'll find that Captain Gower's death is murder. I'm sorry, Miss Davenport, but whether you like it or not, I believe your school will soon become a crime scene."

"Where are you taking me, Evelyn?" Tommy asked.

"Let us go look at the kittens I spoke about earlier." Tommy stopped walking. He trusted his wife, but he could not understand why she wanted to show him kittens when he was completely certain there was a murder to solve. "The stables are behind the school. It isn't exactly what one would call secluded, but it is certainly much quieter than the school buildings. There's much less chance of us being disturbed, or overheard."

He shook his head. "Why didn't you just tell me that? Instead of waffling about kittens. I thought you'd quite lost your mind, darling."

Evelyn looked at him steadily. "Have you ever known me to lose my mind?"

Tommy blinked, suitably chastened. "No, dear. Now lead the way."

He loved Evelyn for everything that she was. She was a wonderful wife and an attentive and caring mother. But it was when she was sleuthing that he thought he loved her most. She was formidable, brooked no argument with anyone, including him, and was quite brilliant at discerning real clues from a jumble of seemingly unrelated information and items.

"Now, Tommy," Evelyn began, "we must put the Wilfred Owen book back where we found it."

He shook his head. "We can't do that. It has the codes in it. We need them."

"I think we should copy the codes for our own reference and put the book back. Otherwise, it is not playing fair with the police. We must give them the same opportunity as us to break the code and solve the crime."

"I suppose we should," he agreed.

"We definitely should," Evelyn said firmly. "I don't want the police to refuse to work with us again in the future."

"I thought we weren't sleuthing anymore. Not now that we have a child. I'm sure that's what you said."

"Yes, well," Evelyn replied, her manner a little flustered, "I was quite sure that we shouldn't. Though now we are beginning another investigation, I do realise how very much I should miss it if we stopped investigating and never did it again. We simply must find out who killed Captain Gower."

"I don't care what the staff said about him or his

recent behaviour. There must be a reason for him behaving the way they say he did."

"I'm sure you're right, darling. The doctor will be here soon, and he will give his opinion regarding the escalation of Mr Gower's death. What should our plan of action be?"

"I think we need to speak properly to Bertie Adams. We have looked around Ralph's apartment. I think we should also look around his classroom. Miss Davenport said he was working in his classroom on something and refused to share details of what he was working on. That could be relevant."

"Yes, I think that's correct. That is a good start. Perhaps we will find some more clues there. Or at the very least, get an idea of Mr Gower's state of mind. Perhaps the way he kept his classroom will help there. If it is extremely orderly, like his apartment, then it's less likely his behaviour was because of some sort of breakdown."

Tommy nodded his agreement. "Then who should we speak to?"

"We need to gather more information," Evelyn said. "Definitely Bertie Adams, as we've already said. Miss Davenport, Miss Cambridge. I would also suggest Nanny Bunting. She seems like the sort of person who knows everything."

"What about the maid, Daisy? She seems rather a timid little thing. I'm not sure she would be any help, but perhaps we should try."

"We most certainly should," Evelyn said. "Maids see and hear much, much more than people realise. Especially in a house this size."

"Do you say that from experience?"

"Of course," she said. "Doris knows everything. Goodness me, sometimes I'm sure that girl knows things before even I do. As for Mrs O'Connell and Mrs Chapman, there isn't a thing that goes on in our house that she doesn't know. One should never neglect or dismiss the knowledge of one's staff as not being relevant."

"I see. I suppose I'd never really thought of it that way. But you are the expert on these matters, my dear." Evelyn looked around as they approached the stable block. "What are you looking for?"

"I suppose there should be a groom somewhere around here, shouldn't there?"

"I would think so," he replied. "Why are you looking for a groom?"

"As we have just discussed, darling, one should never underestimate the knowledge of staff. They could have crucial information without even realising how important it is." Evelyn looked towards the stables in front of them, keen to speak to the groom and then hurry back to Ralph Gower's room so they could be there in time to speak to the doctor.

They walked around the stable block, eventually finding a man pushing a wheelbarrow towards one of the empty stalls. "Excuse me," Evelyn called. "May we speak with you?"

The man turned and took off his cap as they approached. "Good morning."

"Good morning," Tommy replied as he stepped forward with an outstretched hand. "We are Lord and Lady Northmoor. We are here to register our daughter's name at the school."

"How wonderful," the man replied as he accepted Tommy's handshake. "It is a pleasure to meet you, Lord Northmoor. How may I help you this morning?"

"I hoped to speak to you about the terrible tragedy that has befallen the school."

"Tragedy?" the man echoed with a frown. "Oh, do forgive me. I've not introduced myself. My name is Frank Mitchell and I'm the head groom here at Docere House."

Tommy inclined his head at the other's introduction, then moved swiftly on. "Sadly, the science master, Captain Ralph Gower, has been found dead."

He hated the bald words that sounded overly harsh, and were still incomprehensible to him, even as he said them.

"Oh, no. Now that is a horrible shame, my lord," the groom replied. "I particularly liked the fellow."

"Did you know him well?" Tommy asked.

"Yes, indeed. Whenever Mr Gower felt overwhelmed by his duties at the school, he would come down to the stables. He liked the fresh air, and he said the horses reminded him of his time in the army. Now, it probably isn't for me to say, but I believe that he found those days, those dark, dark days as hard as they were, a time when he did something purposeful."

"And you don't think that he felt the same about teaching here at the school?"

The groom gave Tommy what could only be described as a measured look. "It's not quite the same, is it, my lord? Teaching rich, privileged children is hardly the same at all as doing something which you believe can affect the outcome of a war."

"Did Captain Gower share what his duties were during his service time?" Tommy asked sharply.

"Absolutely not," the groom said in an equally abrupt tone. He then seemed to remember to whom he was speaking. "Apologies for my brusque tone, my lord. Mr Gower wasn't like that. He was a good man and would never have shared the confidential details of his service. However, he told me enough that I was certain he made a very great difference to the war effort."

"Of course, apologies for suggesting such a

thing," Tommy said contritely. "Captain Gower was an honourable man. I should have known better than to even think that he would share specific information about his duties."

Tommy breathed in deeply, trying to calm his racing thoughts. He could understand why Ralph had found this spot tranquil. There was nothing like the sound of birds, the smell of animals, and the sight of vast swathes of green grass to make one feel as though the world was not full of anger, violence, and utter heartbreak.

"If I may enquire, what happened to Mr Gower? I saw him only a couple of days ago. He seemed his normal self."

"It seems he had some tummy trouble," Evelyn said delicately, "and that escalated. Earlier today he was found deceased in his room."

"I'm so sorry to hear that." The groom shook his head sadly. "I will miss our chats."

"Have you noticed anything peculiar about the Captain recently?" Tommy asked.

"Peculiar? How so, my lord?"

"Talking to himself. Perhaps being a little nervous in disposition."

The groom gave a laugh that he quickly realised was not entirely appropriate. "Again, apologies. I mean no disrespect, but Captain Gower often spoke to himself. He was rather a whizz. I often find that his type of intelligent fellow goes around talking to themselves as though they're solving the world's problems, while the rest of us just carry on our everyday lives."

"So you don't think it was unusual to see Captain Gower talking to himself around the grounds of Docere House?"

"Not unusual, no. Not for Captain Gower, at any rate. As to a nervous disposition, I would say no. I can't say that I saw anything like that either. However, there is one thing that perhaps may be relevant that you may wish to know."

"Do tell," Tommy said with some urgency. "Anything that is out of the ordinary could be of the utmost importance."

"I don't understand." The groom cast a speculative look at Tommy and Evelyn. "How could Captain Gower's behaviour possibly be connected to his untimely death from a stomach complaint?"

"We might as well tell him, Tommy," Evelyn said gently. "The police are here. It will not be long before people realise that there may be something more to Captain Gower's death than a sad demise."

"Oh my goodness gracious me," the groom said quickly. "Are you suggesting that poor Captain Gower may have been murdered?"

Tommy held up a hand. "That is not for us to say. The police are here, as my wife has said, and it is their job to investigate. First, to find out if a crime has taken place, and second, if they decide that it has, to apprehend the perpetrator. I am simply here as an old comrade of Captain Gower's, wishing to know a little more about his life before he passed away."

"I see," the groom replied. "That makes sense, my lord. Now, the incident to which I earlier referred was an argument that I witnessed between Captain Gower and the young lady who assists Miss Davenport."

"You mean Clarissa Cambridge?" Evelyn asked.

"Yes, that's her. Pretty little thing. A fellow tends to notice where Miss Cambridge is when she is out and about in the grounds of the school."

"Yes," Tommy said. "I can see that. Now, you say an argument?"

"Yes," the groom said slowly. "As I say, I noticed Miss Cambridge and then Captain Gower came out of his building and joined Miss Cambridge."

"Did this seem to be a planned meeting?" Evelyn asked.

"I wouldn't have said so, my lady. It seemed that Miss Cambridge was simply taking a walk. Mr Gower perhaps saw her from his room and came rushing out of the building and chased after her. She seemed quite startled when he approached her."

Evelyn said with a nod. "I imagine so. It must have been quite a shock for her to find him rushing up behind her."

"Yes, indeed," the groom said. "That is what I thought."

"It looked as though she was trying to placate him. There were a lot of hand gestures and pats on the arm. However, it seemed that everything she said made him angrier."

"Was that unusual for him?" Tommy asked. "To chase after a young woman in an apparently agitated way?"

"Almost definitely. He was a very even-tempered chap."

"Prior to that incident, I wouldn't have thought anything could rile him up like that. But on this occasion, something that Miss Cambridge had done, or said, clearly had."

"I see," Tommy said. "Do you have an opinion on what the conflict could have been about?"

"It probably isn't for me to say."

"Perhaps not," Tommy agreed. "But please, say it anyway."

"I did get the feeling that perhaps it was something of a personal nature. A lover's tiff, if you will."

"Ah," Tommy said. "They are two young people working together in a relatively secluded environment. It's entirely possible that they were interested in each other romantically."

"Of course it's possible," Evelyn added. "But is it likely?"

"I don't see why not," Tommy said. "Of course,

there is a rather an age gap, but that's not entirely unusual."

"Ten to fifteen years or so isn't very unusual these days, my lord," the groom said. "Not when Captain Gower worked long hours here at the school and had little opportunity to go into the village."

"I wonder if Miss Davenport was aware." Evelyn mused.

Frank Mitchell gazed at Evelyn in dismay. "Please don't repeat what I said. I would hate to be wrong and to get young Miss Cambridge into any trouble. She's a very sweet girl."

"You can rest assured we won't repeat our conversation with anyone," Tommy said. "Now, one last thing. Is it possible for me to borrow a pencil and a piece of paper?"

"Wouldn't it be simpler to get those things from Miss Davenport?" the groom asked doubtfully.

"It certainly would," Tommy agreed. "However, I do not want Miss Davenport to know what I am doing. Perhaps this could also remain between us?"

"How curious." The groom beckoned them with a crooked finger. "Follow me and I will furnish you with a pencil and paper. If you don't mind my saying so, this is beginning to feel a little like we are in the middle of one of those Sherlock Holmes novels."

While Tommy could certainly appreciate what the groom meant and even understand the other man's increasing excitement, this wasn't at all like fiction to him. It was very real. The sense of foreboding that had come over him when he arrived at Docere House had increased exponentially.

Somewhere among this seemingly serene countryside school was a cold-blooded murderer. He could only hope that they could apprehend the perpetrator before anyone else was hurt.

4

Evelyn followed Tommy back towards Ralph's rooms. As they reached the building, Julia Davenport approached from the direction of the main school, accompanied by a man. If it were not immediately obvious from the black bag that he carried, then it was clear from his demeanour that he was the village doctor. The man was middle-aged, wore a smart black hat, yet looked harried and walked as though he was used to rushing everywhere he went.

"Good morning, I'm Lord Northmoor," Tommy said. "I assume you are Dr Brady?"

The man took off his hat as he glanced at Evelyn. "Pleased to meet you, even though it is under these difficult circumstances. Good day to you, Lady Northmoor."

"Are you the same physician that attended Captain Gower earlier today?"

Dr Brady inclined his head. "That is correct."

"Where have you been?" Julia Davenport interrupted, eyeing Tommy and Evelyn with suspicion.

"To the stables." Evelyn blinked innocently. "We are a couple of mousers short at Hessleham Hall and I wanted to enquire as to the availability of the kittens that you have. Our chauffeur mentioned there was a couple that I may want to look at."

The headmistress looked at Evelyn with obvious disbelief, but she did not challenge the veracity of her statement.

They all climbed the stairs to Ralph's rooms without further conversation. The doctor paused outside the bedroom of the dead man. "Would you all wait here, please?"

Evelyn didn't think the headmistress would need asking twice—the other woman's face had turned positively green. She busied herself looking at a painting on the wall opposite the dead teacher's bookshelf while waiting for the doctor to complete his examination of Ralph's body. Julia came over to join her.

"It's rather provincial."

"I quite like it," Evelyn replied as she peered closer, trying to distinguish the signature in the bottom right corner.

"It's not to my taste," the headmistress said dismissively.

Evelyn felt, rather than heard, Tommy moving towards the bookcase behind them as they spoke. She endeavoured to keep Julia's attention diverted while Tommy replaced the poetry book on the shelf.

"Do you know who painted this picture?"

"Yes, I do. It was Ralph Gower himself."

Tommy strode over to join them. Evelyn glanced behind her and saw that the Wilfred Owen book was pulled out slightly from the other books, just as it had been when they discovered it earlier that morning.

The painting was of Docere House, and associated buildings. Ralph had even added a couple of horses in the background. Although it was clearly an amateur painting, Evelyn thought it rather sweet.

"I didn't know he could paint." Tommy pulled a hand through his hair. "How did I not know that he could paint?"

Evelyn had tried to tell her husband earlier that although Tommy knew the person Ralph had been during their time together at army training, he knew little about who he had been in the years immediately preceding his death.

Truth be told, Tommy didn't know much about Ralph's work during the war either, only what they had found on his friend's service record.

Dr Brady joined them in the sitting room. "I wouldn't have expected gastroenteritis to progress so quickly, and I certainly wouldn't have expected it to result in the death of what appears to be a previously healthy man."

"What do you suspect, doctor?" Tommy asked. "Is it possible he could have been poisoned?"

Dr Brady pulled out a handkerchief and wiped it across his brow. It wasn't a particularly warm day, and other than climbing the stairs, he'd done nothing strenuous that could have caused him to perspire. He was patently giving himself a moment to think of a suitable response to Tommy's forthright question.

"It's possible," he said shortly. "At this point, I believe nothing can be ruled in or out."

"Please don't allow yourself to jump to conclusions, Lord Northmoor," Julia Davenport urged.

"I shall arrange to have the body removed for further examination." The doctor addressed the headmistress.

"I refuse to believe this has anything to do with the school," Julia declared loudly. "This must be something to do with the secret work he was doing. We must keep Docere House out of any newspaper reports about Mr Gower's death."

Evelyn reached out and put a hand on Tommy's arm to pacify him as she spoke. "I understand your reluctance for adverse publicity, Miss

Davenport. However, I cannot see how it can be avoided."

"If he hadn't been so intent on hiding away in his laboratory working on some project that he was determined to keep secret, this would never have happened," the headmistress snapped.

"What are you saying?" Tommy rounded on Miss Davenport, his face a mask of pure fury. "That Ralph deserved what happened to him?"

Julia held up a hand as though to ward off Tommy, even though he hadn't taken a single step towards her. "Calm down, Lord Northmoor."

Her tone was pure headmistress—all control and repressed frustration.

"One of your teachers is lying in that room next door, dead," he said. "You are now saying that the work he was doing had something to do with his death. A death which, may I say, is suspicious. Dr Brady has told us that. I don't know how you can remain so composed. Someone at your school must be a killer."

"No one here can possibly be responsible for what happened to Mr Gower."

"You can't know that," Evelyn said. "None of us can know that."

"My staff are thoroughly vetted before being given a position here," Julia said stiffly. "I am not in the habit of employing people who may commit murder."

"And yet," Tommy said with a glance towards the open bedroom door where Ralph lay, "Captain Gower is, in fact, dead. The doctor believes that a simple stomach complaint would not have caused his death. It must therefore have been caused by someone. Face facts, Miss Davenport, this is a murder."

The headmistress drew in a deep breath, which suggested she was not nearly as calm as she appeared. "Perhaps it was some sort of accident."

"My dear lady." The doctor mopped his brow once more. "I can assure you that my medical opinion is sound. I have already stated that it is possible..."

"Yes, yes," Julia interrupted. "You think poison, as suggested by Lord Northmoor, is possible, but you cannot rule out him dying from gastroenteritis, can you?"

"It is not for me to anticipate the findings of the postmortem. Let us leave the adjudication of the poor fellow's death to an expert."

"If you were pushed to give your opinion, doctor, what would it be?" A thread of pure steel ran through Tommy's voice as he addressed the doctor directly. "Unofficially, of course."

"Let me speak plainly," Dr Brady answered, with a swift glance towards Miss Davenport. "I am as certain as I can be that the unfortunate chap was hastened to his death by another person. That is not my medical opinion, as I do not have enough evidence, but it's my personal belief. Make of that what you will."

Tommy and Evelyn said their goodbyes to Dr Brady and got directions from Julia to Ralph's classroom. The classrooms were on the floor below those of the schoolmasters.

Tommy was not surprised to see Bertie Adams pottering at the desk when he entered the classroom that had once been Ralph's. The desk was at the front of the room, directly underneath a large blackboard.

"Hello," Bertie said hesitatingly.

Tommy nodded towards the other man. "Mr Adams, I apologise that I don't have time for social niceties. I simply must get to the bottom of what happened to Captain Gower. Do you have any idea what secret work he was doing?"

"Absolutely not, Lord Northmoor," Mr Adams said with no hesitation. "He didn't share any of the details of his work with me. That was the reason Miss Davenport was angry with him. Well, perhaps not angry. That is too strong a word. Frustrated. Yes, that's better. She was frustrated with him."

The man was babbling again. Tommy reined in his own irritation at the science master's manner. It was really no wonder Ralph shared nothing with Bertie Adams. "Why do you think that was?"

"Well, I should say because he was using his classroom and school facilities to conduct a private or personal experiment. Otherwise, why would he not just simply say what he was doing?"

"How did Miss Davenport know Captain Gower was doing experiments in his classroom that were not work related?" Evelyn asked as she leaned against the desk.

"I...that is...several of us were concerned about Mr Gower." Bertie Adams swallowed audibly. "That is...um...Captain Gower's health. It seemed to go downhill at the same time as he became more secretive."

"You told her, didn't you?" Tommy could not keep the accusatory tone from his voice.

"It was my duty," Bertie said in a weaselly voice. "Don't you see? He was using school property in a personal capacity. That isn't allowed."

"How do you know that Captain Gower wasn't researching a cure for tuberculosis, or something similar?"

"He wasn't," Bertie stated flatly. "He was doing something furtive."

"Did you ever ask him specifically what he was doing?"

"Yes, I did, Lady Northmoor. I asked him outright on several occasions what it was he was doing, and he refused to tell me. Not only that, but he refused to allow me to assist him." Tommy noticed Bertie calmed considerably when talking to Evelyn rather than to himself. "Part of his role as a senior master was to allow me to help him. Oh, he allowed me to assist him when he was teaching or marking schoolwork or setting prep. Those types of administration work he was more than happy to share with me. After several weeks of him shutting me out of his work, I spoke to Miss Davenport."

Tommy strode over to the window and peered out. All he could see were the soft hills and valleys of the North Yorkshire countryside. Usually, such a sight would both calm and ground him. However, on this occasion, he thought nothing was ever going to make him feel tranquil ever again.

As he was turning away from the window, something snagged Tommy's attention. He turned back and gazed out again, trying to see what his subconscious had noticed. It took him a few moments before he saw a group of red berries on the windowsill. The building was far enough away from trees that it wasn't possible the berries could have blown onto the windowsill or landed there by any means other than being placed there.

He pulled up the sash window and reached out to take the berries. As he did so, he realised there was a scrap of paper underneath them. Hearing footsteps behind him, he adjusted the angle of his body so he could grab both the berries and the paper without his action being seen clearly.

"What is it?" Bertie asked from close behind him.

Tommy transferred the berries into his left hand and turned to face the science master with that hand outstretched. He put his other hand into his trouser pocket. "Do you know what these are?"

"Yes, of course," Bertie replied. "They are berries from a yew tree. We have several in the grounds."

"What are they used for?"

Bertie laughed nervously. "One doesn't use them for anything, Lord Northmoor, though you can eat them if you wish. So long as you don't eat the stone in the centre—that is extremely toxic."

"Isn't the yew tree itself poisonous?" Evelyn asked with a frown. "I seem to remember our gardener telling me that when I came across him destroying one in the grounds of Hessleham Hall."

"That is correct, Lady Northmoor. You would have to ingest the parts that are poisonous, but I'm sure the berries would look very attractive to children. Your gardener has done the right thing by demolishing the tree you had in your grounds."

Tommy looked at his hand in mild dismay. "But the berries are safe?"

"That's right. No harm will come to you, Lord Northmoor, unless you decide to eat the berries and then chew on the stones inside."

Tommy didn't like the almost gleeful expression that crossed Bertie Adams's face as he delivered the last few words. He was almost afraid to ask his next question, but he needed to know the answer. "What are the effects of yew tree poisoning?"

"Headache, stomach cramps, nausea, and vomiting."

"All signs exhibited by Captain Gower," Tommy said grimly.

"Yes. But of course, those are also the signs of gastroenteritis."

"What else can you tell me about the yew tree?"

"History tells us that Boudicea actually ingested yew leaves after she lost in battle to the Romans. Evidently, she preferred suicide to being taken prisoner. The poisonous part of the plant is known as taxine. No one in their right mind would deliberately eat yew leaves, or any other part of the plant."

"Are you suggesting Captain Gower was not in his right mind?"

"Nothing of the sort," Bertie said. "His behaviour was a little odd, but I can't imagine that he would deliberately hurt himself."

"And if someone wished to hurt him?" Tommy pressed. "Could they do so?"

"I shouldn't have thought so," Bertie said dismissively. "The only person in the school likely to know how to turn the taxine into either liquid or powder form was Mr Gower himself. He was an exceptionally clever scientist."

"It would seem rather a stretch for him to go to the trouble to make either, only to use it to kill himself." Tommy put the berries onto the desk and rubbed at the back of his neck thoughtfully. "Surely if he wanted to harm himself, he would simply eat the leaves or chew the stone from the berries."

"You are certain that if someone wished to cause Mr Gower's death, there is no one here at the school with the skill required to turn the taxine into either liquid or powder form so that it could be administered without him being suspicious?" Evelyn asked.

"That is correct, Lady Northmoor."

Tommy frowned. Why would Ralph have left the berries on the windowsill with a scrap of paper, unless it was some sort of message? He wanted Bertie out of the classroom so he could look at the paper in his pocket. Tommy expected it to contain numbers and letters, like the ones that they had found in the margins of the book of poetry.

"I wonder," he said. "May we have some time alone here in Ralph's classroom? I suddenly feel rather close to him here and I would like to have a little privacy."

"Of course, Lord Northmoor." Bertie bowed his head. "You can find me over in the main school building should you wish to ask me any other questions."

Evelyn followed Bertie over to the door and ensured it was closed firmly behind the science master before turning to Tommy. “What have you found?”

“How do you know I’ve found anything?”

“Thomas Christie,” Evelyn said with a sidelong look at her husband. “We have been married long enough for me to know when there is something you are hiding. Now, what is it?”

“There was a piece of paper under the berries.” Tommy pulled it out of his pocket and held it out to her.

“What can all these numbers and letters mean?”

“I don’t know.” Tommy sighed deeply. “But I fear we must find out, and quickly. Ralph has clearly left this as another clue. He has more faith in me than I have in myself. He clearly believed this was a code that we could crack.”

Evelyn put a hand over Tommy’s. “We can, darling. I am absolutely sure of that.”

The code with the berries:

J3:12,9

P58:4,2

R20:12,14

"Hello," Evelyn said conversationally. "It's Daisy, isn't it?"

"Yes, my lady, that's right," the young maid responded. "How may I help you?

"I wonder...I apologise, and I hope this isn't too much of an imposition." Evelyn smiled reassuringly at the girl. "I just wondered who I should ask about getting a tea tray."

"Why, I would be happy to get that for you, Lady Northmoor. Is it tea for one or two?"

"Oh, tea for one, yes please, and if it isn't too much trouble, I'm sure my husband would very much appreciate a pot of coffee?" Evelyn waved a hand toward the front door of Docere House. "He's off exploring somewhere. I'm not exactly sure where he's gone. I'm afraid when he gets a mind to it, he goes on rather energetic walks. It's a little too much for me to keep up with him."

Daisy seemed to realise immediately what Evelyn was hinting at. "Perhaps you'd like to sit down, Lady Northmoor."

"Could I?" Evelyn asked. "Oh, that would be simply glorious."

"Follow me," Daisy said and walked along the corridor in the opposite direction to Miss Davenport's office. "Miss Davenport put the police in here, but they've also gone off exploring, looking for clues, I should expect."

"Of course," Evelyn said. "Lord Northmoor and I

have known the two detectives for some time. The detective inspector is such a clever man. I'm sure he'll get to the bottom of what's going on in no time at all."

Daisy led Evelyn into a very comfortable sitting room. "This is where parents wait if Miss Davenport is unavoidably detained. Not that that happens very often. She's extremely punctual and well organised."

"It's an exceptionally lovely room." Evelyn looked around with admiration as she took a seat on the large brown leather Chesterfield sofa.

Daisy glanced anxiously towards the door, as though afraid of being overheard. "That is to say, I think it's Nanny Bunting who is the organised one. She has the entire school running just the way she wants it. Everyone, including Miss Davenport, dances to Nanny Bunting's tune."

"How simply marvellous. I have a similar paragon at Hessleham Hall that I rely on. Mrs Chapman runs the entire house and rarely needs me to do a thing. I am exceedingly lucky."

Daisy bobbed her knee. "I shall see about that tea, my lady."

"I wonder," Evelyn said, glancing over to the door, "might you just close that door for a moment and could we perhaps have a little conversation?"

Daisy looked doubtfully at Evelyn as though she couldn't think of a single thing about which they could converse, but also could think of no way of politely refusing. “One moment, my lady.”

The maid shut the door and hurried back across the room to stand in front of Evelyn. She was so close that Evelyn could see the girl’s whole body was trembling, as though she was terrified that she had done something wrong and was standing in front of a firing squad instead of Evelyn herself.

“Now Daisy, please calm yourself,” Evelyn said firmly. “You have done absolutely nothing wrong and I only wish to ask you a couple of quick questions. Then I would be very grateful if you could see about the tea tray.”

“Of course, Lady Northmoor.” The girl licked her lips, but her anxiety did not seem to diminish.

“Can you tell me if you know anything at all about Captain Gower? That is Mr Ralph Gower, the Science Master, who has unfortunately died this morning.”

“Oh, I was so sad to hear about that, Lady Northmoor. He was such a nice man.”

Evelyn wondered if, in fact, the girl knew him to be a nice man or whether Daisy was just saying the sort of thing that one said when someone died. “Was he? Was he a nice man?”

“Oh yes, Lady Northmoor,” Daisy said quickly, “Some of the Masters have no time for people like me. I’m just a house servant, you see, but Mr Gower, he wasn’t like that. He would often ask how I was—

as though he really meant it, you understand. He even asked about my mother."

"Your mother?" Evelyn smiled kindly, glad the girl had forgotten her nerves, and was talking with little hint of any reservation.

"She's been rather unwell. I was a little upset a couple of weeks ago and Mr Gower saw that and asked what the matter was."

"And you told him?"

"Yes." Daisy twisted her hands together in front of her. "Perhaps I shouldn't have done. Maybe it wasn't the right thing to do, but he did ask."

"That was very kind of him," Evelyn said, "and then afterwards, some time later, he asked if she was any better?"

"Yes he did. That's why I say he was a kind man. Nobody else even realised there was anything wrong with me, but he did."

"Is there anything else that you can think of? Any other little incidents that you can tell me about?"

"Well," Daisy hesitated and bit her lip, then gave a brief nod as though reassuring herself that it was alright to carry on talking to Evelyn. "Last week he was talking to Miss Davenport. I probably shouldn't repeat this. Maybe I've got it wrong. Maybe I didn't hear it correctly."

"Tell me what you heard," Evelyn said quietly. "Don't worry about whether you recall the conversation word for word. I shan't repeat anything that you tell me. It will stay between us."

"Well, as I say," Daisy continued. "Miss Davenport had asked me to bring in a tea tray, and I'd gone to fetch it. When I returned, I ordinarily, you see, just knock on the door and go straight in, but as I approached the door, I could hear raised voices, and I wasn't quite certain whether I should go in or wait."

"Oh dear, how very awkward for you."

"Well, yes, it was rather."

"What did you do?"

"I waited," Daisy said. "I waited outside with the tray."

"And is this when you heard, or thought you heard, something that you are now not sure about?"

"Well, I am sure," Daisy said then, and her chin raised a notch. "That's the thing. I'm very sure of what I heard. I heard it very distinctly. The problem is that it makes no sense. That's why I am worried I heard it incorrectly."

"What was it you heard? Try to remember as accurately as you can." Evelyn leaned forward.

"Mr Gower said to Miss Davenport that it was a matter of national security."

"What was?"

"Oh, I don't know," Daisy said. "I didn't hear that part. I just heard Mr Gower in an extremely loud voice saying that Miss Davenport was putting national security at risk. I can't imagine what he could have meant by that. The war's over, isn't it?"

"Well, yes. Yes, it is," Evelyn agreed. "Quite over, thank goodness."

"That's what I thought," Daisy said. "That's why it seemed such a curious turn of phrase."

"Did you hear anything else?"

"No. No." The girl's hands stopped twisting together and her whole body seemed to sag in relief as though she were glad to have shared this burden with someone else. "At that point, Miss Bunting gave me a very sharp look, and I knocked on the door and took the tea tray straight in."

"Yes. Yes, I see." Evelyn smiled kindly at the girl. "Well, thank you Daisy. Thank you for sharing that with me and for trusting me with that information."

Relief flooded through the girl's body, and she hurried towards the door. "I'll go see about that tray for you now. Tea for one and coffee for Lord Northmoor ready for when he comes back."

"Thank you, Daisy."

5

Clarissa Cambridge was in the library when Tommy found her. The library was in the main Docere House building at the opposite end to Julia Davenport's office. It was a large room with picture windows that overlooked the grounds. Shelves of books lined three walls of the room. A large mantlepiece stood on the wall to the left of the doorway, dominated by lion's head ornaments on each end.

Miss Davenport's attractive blonde assistant had her back to Tommy as he walked into the large room. "Miss Cambridge, I wonder if I might have a few moments of your time?"

The assistant jumped as though Tommy had clanged a bell in her ear. When she turned to face him, one hand rested on her chest as though she were trying to calm a rapidly beating heart. "Lord Northmoor, you scared me!"

"I apologise." He smiled in his most charming manner. "I should have realised you would be on edge following Captain Gower's death."

She raised an eyebrow. "Not particularly."

"His passing must have been quite a shock."

"Of course," she replied. "But a death from a stomach complaint, no matter how tragic or unexpected, is hardly the sort of thing that would put one on edge."

He wondered for a moment what would make the unruffled assistant nervous, but then he already knew one possible answer to that conundrum—entering a room quietly while a person has their back to the door would do it nearly every time. Was that the only thing that had startled her? His feet made no sound on the thick carpet that ran down the centre of the hallway outside the library, and he hadn't cleared his throat to announce his presence or made any other sound. Tommy supposed talking to her from the hallway instead of entering the room would have alarmed her less. He should probably learn more about the headmistress's assistant before he based his suspicions on the way she had, in his opinion, so cavalierly dismissed Ralph's demise.

Tommy stepped into the room and looked over Clarissa's shoulder at the shelf of books in front of her. If this were one of the books his sister Grace loved to read, Clarissa would be looking at a book that detailed how to make taxine. Or, at the very least, a volume that would point to another clue that Ralph had left for him. Of course, neither of those things happened in real life. The books in front of the assistant seemed to be nonfiction and on a range of subjects—none of which was science.

"Looking for something in particular?"

"Yes." Clarissa gazed at him steadily. "Miss Davenport asked me to do some research for her."

"Can I help?"

She gave a small shrug. "If you like. I thought you would be busy sleuthing."

"Did you?" This time it was Tommy's turn to give Clarissa a searching gaze. "Why would you think that?"

"Miss Davenport told me that you and Lady Northmoor have done a little investigating of your own in the past."

Tommy did his best not to show annoyance at the term 'a little'. He and Evelyn had helped the police on several occasions now, their efforts catching several murderers. He kept his tone even. "We do our best."

"I'm sure," she replied. "Now, how can I help you? I assume you have come to talk to me as a witness. Or am I considered a suspect?"

The last sentence was delivered with a deliberate light and casual air, but Tommy was not fooled. The woman was concerned. Was it simply because she was innocent and was worried about how to prove it, or did she have something to hide? "Miss Davenport will tell you that we consider everyone a suspect until we have evidence to show otherwise."

"Even Miss Davenport herself?"

"Everyone," he reiterated. "Regardless of who they are or what their role was in Captain Gower's life."

"Why are you so keen to believe his death was murder?"

"Why are you so eager to believe it was not?"

"Touché, Lord Northmoor."

He decided against telling Miss Cambridge what the doctor had said. Either the police or Miss Davenport would do that. "How well did you know Captain Gower?"

"Not as well as you," she replied. "I didn't even know he had been in the army before coming to work here."

"You didn't talk about that?"

"We didn't talk about much," she replied. "We were colleagues but didn't choose to spend time with each other on a personal level."

Tommy walked over to the window and looked outside, then at the windowsill. He half expected to find some other clue there, but there was nothing to see but the white painted wood. "I've already spoken to someone who says Captain Gower rushed after you and you shared what appeared to be a heated discussion. Perhaps that was about budget concerns, or some other school issue?"

She looked away and bit her lip. "I didn't want to have to tell you the whole sorry truth, but it appears I must."

Tommy's palms felt sweaty, but he resisted rubbing them on his trousers. Miss Davenport's demeanour and the great reluctance in her voice told him that what she was about to reveal would not be pleasant to hear. "Please tell me the truth."

Clarissa Cambridge lifted a hand and toyed with the chain of her necklace. Slowly, she looked back at him, heat staining her cheeks. "Mr Gower had been pursuing me."

"Personally?"

"Yes," she said. "Very personally. It was getting to where I had threatened to tell Miss Davenport if he did not stop."

Tommy thought carefully before asking his next question. He didn't want to know the answer, but there again, what the assistant had to tell him could help the investigation. "Was he pressing his attention on you against your will?"

"Nothing quite so dramatic, Lord Northmoor." Clarissa gave him a small but reassuring smile. "He asked me to go to the pictures with him. Or to a dance. The venue changed but his perseverance did not. It didn't seem to matter how many times I told him no, he simply would not stop asking me. He was becoming more persistent and disinclined to hear the word no."

"I'm very sorry to hear that. Captain Gower always seemed to be a very honourable man."

"People change," Clarissa said with a wistful tone. "I know better than most."

Tommy wished people would stop telling him that Ralph was different from the person he knew during their training. He knew that. He himself was a much different man, and husband, after the war to the one who had gone away to fight. Was it possible, despite his deep-set beliefs, that Ralph's personality had been completely transformed and he was capable of things that he never would've dreamed of? Tommy knew the answer to that rhetorical question, but he didn't want to face it as fact.

"You sound as though you are speaking from experience."

"My husband..." Clarissa said as she fiddled with her necklace.

"You're married?" Incredulity coated each of the three syllables.

"I was," she clarified. "I don't suppose one can claim that descriptor if one's husband is dead."

She did not look old enough to be a war widow. However, the desperation of war meant plenty of couples had got married at a much earlier age than they ordinarily might have. Parents, once reluctant to give their offspring permission for early marriage, were persuaded by imminent departure to war. "I'm very sorry. If it's not too painful for you, where did you lose your husband?"

Clarissa's lips twisted into a sardonic smile. "In our kitchen."

"I'm afraid I don't understand," he said, even as the icy fingers of dread danced across his spine—he had a growing, and horrifying, realisation of where this conversation was going.

"My husband never recovered from what he saw during his time serving his country. Fred took his own life shortly after returning home."

"I'm very sorry to hear that, Miss Cambridge." Tommy frowned. "Have we been under a misapprehension? Should we address you as Mrs Cambridge?"

"No." She stared at a spot over Tommy's shoulder. "Cambridge is my maiden name. I reverted to it when I came back to Docere House. Everyone here knew me as Clarissa Cambridge, so it made more sense than using my married name."

"Is this common knowledge at the school?"

Clarissa Cambridge blinked away tears. "It is not. Miss Davenport knows, of course. I wrote to her after Fred died and asked her if she had a position here at the school she could consider me for. I wanted to leave the area in which we lived and start again. Our home held too many painful memories for me."

"And so here you are," Tommy said. "You're happy here, I hope?"

"Yes, I am." The response was so quick and immediate that Tommy had no trouble believing that Docere House was a haven for the headmistress's assistant. "I always remembered my schooldays fondly. I was head girl here, you know."

"Perhaps you remember my sisters? Constance and Grace Christie. I believe they are a similar age to yourself."

Clarissa's brow furrowed. "No, I don't think that I do."

Tommy made a mental note to ask his sisters if they remembered Clarissa. Any information they could give Tommy may be useful in helping him understand Miss Cambridge better and assessing her character as a possible murderess. "No matter. I shall leave you to your research."

She reached out an arm but stopped short of touching Tommy. "There's one thing that it might help you to know, Lord Northmoor."

"Oh? What is that?"

"Francis Galbraith, one of our maths masters, had a quite terrible row with Mr Gower only yesterday."

"Really? Do you know what about?"

"No, I don't," Miss Cambridge said demurely as she lowered her gaze.

"But you have an idea?"

"I wouldn't wish to speak out of turn," she said. "But I rather have the impression that it had something to do with me."

"I see," Tommy replied, though he didn't really. Not unless there was some sort of love triangle. Stranger things had happened, and he resolved to add the teacher to the list of people he needed to speak to. "Thank you for letting me know."

She seemed to be as aware as Tommy that their conversation was over. She frowned as she looked at the bookcase. "I had better get back to work. Miss Davenport will wonder what is keeping me."

"Of course." Tommy inclined his head slightly. "Thank you for speaking to me."

"Lady Northmoor." Julia Davenport put the cap on her pen and laid it next to one of the piles of paper on her desk. It was so chaotic it looked as though several storms had blown through the room leaving a haphazard trail of documents in its wake. "How can I help you?"

"I wonder if I might ask you what you may think is an intrusive question?" Evelyn's heart rate increased—she was about to take a gamble that may or may not pay off. It might also make Tommy rather cross with her.

The headmistress sighed, making no attempt to hide her frustration. "I suppose if you feel as though you must ask the question, then I will do my best to answer it."

"Thank you." Evelyn licked her lips, then abruptly dropped into one of the empty chairs across the desk from Miss Davenport. "What sort of references do you obtain for your staff before employing them?"

"My staff?" The other woman straightened a pile of papers, then looked at Evelyn with a direct challenge in her eyes. "Are you asking as an amateur sleuth or as a parent of a prospective pupil?"

"Both," Evelyn said promptly. "Why? Would your response be different depending on under which capacity I am asking?"

"Not really," she answered. "I endeavour to obtain two references for each member of staff I employ. At least one usually pertains to the person's skills for the role for which they have applied. Another may be simply a character reference. If you asked as a parent, I would probably tell you we carry out stringent checks, which, of course, we do. I take the safety of our pupils extremely seriously."

"Can you share with me who provided a reference for Captain Gower?"

A pile of papers slid around the desk as Julia

Davenport folded her hands on top of it. "Does Lord Northmoor know you're asking personal questions about his comrade?"

"Does that have any relevance whether or not you'll answer my question?" Evelyn was proud to hear that her voice did not shake one bit—she sounded as confident and in control as Aunt Em herself.

"I don't suppose it does." The headmistress allowed a small smile to form on her lips. "You've changed, Lady Northmoor."

"I shall take that as a compliment," Evelyn said.

"Ralph Gower was given a glowing reference from his university tutor after his two-year course. He then worked at a public school in York as a science master before applying here. Again, his reference from that school was exemplary."

"You didn't receive a reference from the army?"

"I had no reason to request one, Lady Northmoor." Julia Davenport shuffled her papers, found her pen, and twirled it between her fingers. "I had two references pertinent to the role he applied for at Docere House. I had no requirement of another."

"Did you ever have cause to speak to Captain Gower about his time serving in the army?" Evelyn asked, struggling to find a way to ask the headmistress about the comment Daisy had overheard without coming right out and asking, which she did not want to do. She had promised the girl that she would not reveal their conversation to anyone else, and she intended to honour the assurance she had given to the housemaid.

Miss Davenport tapped her pen on the desk. "We had a few conversations generally, but like many men of his ilk, he seemed neither comfortable nor inclined to speak about his service."

Evelyn gave herself a moment to think before forming her next question. What could Ralph's comment about the headteacher putting national security at risk have meant? What could she have done, or spoken about doing, that would have led to him saying those words to her?

With sudden clarity, an idea came to Evelyn's mind. Her decision to ask about references had been correct—but it wasn't Ralph's references, or his own background, that was in doubt. "Is it possible that you have employed someone at Docere House that has sympathies with England's enemies?"

"Lady Northmoor!" Julia Davenport slapped her palms onto the desk and pushed herself to her feet. "You have gone too far. I have just told you that I am extremely careful about obtaining references and who I employ. How dare you suggest that I have been negligent in those duties."

Evelyn met the headmistress's furious gaze without flinching. "I'm sorry to have upset you."

"I'm not at all upset. Simply disappointed." The colour on the woman's cheeks, her rapid breathing, and the way she clenched the edge of the desk told Evelyn she wasn't simply upset—she was positively enraged.

"I apologise regardless," Evelyn murmured.

"Where is that girl?" Miss Davenport made a visible effort to relax and glanced towards the door behind Evelyn as though the person she was expecting would materialise.

"Who? Daisy?"

Julia frowned. "No, Miss Cambridge. I sent her to the library to carry out a very simple research task. It should have taken her a few minutes, but she's been gone longer than twenty minutes."

No doubt the assistant had been waylaid by Tommy. Evelyn decided not to share this information with Miss Davenport—she was already angry enough with Evelyn. "I should let you get on."

"Yes," Miss Davenport replied. "You should. However, I will give the name of another person you would do well to question—Edwin Miller."

"Who is that?"

"He's one of our more senior masters. I'm afraid he had reason to dislike Mr Gower."

Evelyn raised a speculative eyebrow. "How so?"

"Only last week, Mr Gower had reason to speak to me about Mr Miller's performance."

It hadn't escaped Evelyn's notice that although Julia had reacted angrily to the question she had asked about the possibility of one of her staff being an enemy of England, she hadn't actually answered. Was mentioning Mr Miller now her way of answering the question in a roundabout way?

"What had Mr Miller done to concern Captain Gower?"

"Mr Gower reported him to me for excessive drinking. He said it had become an open joke amongst the pupils that Mr Miller kept a flask of brandy in his desk drawer."

"Oh dear, how terrible. Was there any credence to Captain Gower's worries?"

Miss Davenport walked around the desk and opened the door to her office, now seemingly in full control of herself. "Absolutely none that I could find. I carried out a check of Mr Miller's schoolroom myself. I found no evidence of alcohol."

"Perhaps Captain Gower..."

"A teacher of his supposed calibre should know that pupils often make cruel jokes," the headmistress said, looking at Evelyn with what could only be described as derision. "As I have previously stated, Mr Gower's behaviour over the last few weeks was causing both me and other members of staff serious concern."

"I see." Evelyn got to her feet and walked over to the door. "Thank you for your help."

How she kept the sarcasm from her last sentence, Evelyn did not know. She was no nearer to finding out what Ralph had meant when speaking to the headmistress about national security, but she did now have another person it was important she speak with.

~

After some wrong turns, Tommy eventually found his way to the classroom used by the maths master, Francis Galbraith. "You must be Lord Northmoor. Give me one moment and I'll be with you."

Tommy waited outside while the teacher addressed his class. When he closed the door firmly behind Galbraith, Tommy immediately decided he liked the other man. He had red hair, freckles, and an extremely forthright manner, which he couldn't help but admire. "How did you know who I was?"

"Begging your pardon, my lord, but you're the only stranger wandering around Docere House looking as though you want to commit murder to avenge the loss of your fallen pal."

"Gosh," Tommy said. "Do I really look that irate?"

The other man's lips twisted as though he was trying to find the appropriate words to use shortly before he gave up and went with honesty. "Like you could do it with your bare hands."

"Goodness," Tommy replied. "I need to work on my poker face."

The teacher held up a finger. "One moment. Wellesley really needs to remember who he is dealing with here."

Francis Galbraith stuck his head back through the classroom door, caught his assistant's eye, and gesticulated to the rear of the room.

"They look like senior pupils," Tommy commented. "Shouldn't they know better than to cause trouble while you're out of the room?"

"Upper sixth," the teacher confirmed. "Should most certainly know better, but there's a few who do not. Wellesley thinks he's above reproach from anyone. Apart from his Papa, of course."

"Not Roger Wellesley, the government minister, surely?"

"The very same." Francis Galbraith grinned at Tommy. "His son in there will do well to stay out of trouble until after his twenty-first birthday. He does not have the drive, ambition, or control of his father, that's for certain."

The maths teacher's soft Scottish accent contained an equal measure of amusement, derision, and resignation—clearly the lad in question was not only one of the more unruly pupils but also believed to be a lost cause.

"I'd like to ask you a few questions following the death of Captain Gower."

"Of course." The teacher's smile slid off his face,

and he looked soberly at Tommy. "I'll help in any way that I can."

"I understand you had a disagreement with him only yesterday."

The man raised an eyebrow. "I'm surprised you heard about that. It wasn't really an argument, not really."

"Ralph wasn't angry?"

"Oh, he was furious," the maths teacher said.

It was Tommy's turn to look bewildered. "He was furious, but it wasn't an argument?"

"It takes two to argue, Lord Northmoor." The teacher held up both his middle and forefinger, then pushed his middle finger down. "I was not arguing."

"Can you tell me why Captain Gower was angry with you?"

"He warned me to stay away from Miss Cambridge."

"Clarissa Cambridge, the headmistress's assistant?"

"Yes, that's right," he confirmed. "There was really no need for him to warn me away from her."

"But he believed that there was?"

"He most certainly did. He was adamant that I should not get personally involved with her."

"Do you think he was jealous?" Tommy asked.

"Possibly." The maths teacher paused, as though trying to recall the incident clearly. "He said she was dangerous."

"That's an odd choice of words," Tommy said. "Do you think he thought she was some sort of femme fatale?"

"I don't know if it was anything as dramatic as that." The teacher peered through the small window in the door to his classroom, assured himself all was well, and turned back to Tommy. "She's a very sweet girl. Not at all the Mata Hari type, I shouldn't have thought."

"What did he mean by dangerous, then?"

"He told me some story about how her husband had died and if I wasn't careful, I could end up in the ground just like him."

"My goodness. Didn't you believe what he said?"

"I know you were chums with Gower, Lord Northmoor, but I'm afraid I didn't believe a word he said." Francis Galbraith looked apologetically at Tommy. "I thought Gower seemed a little unhinged. He was very insistent and, as I said to you earlier, there was no need for him to warn me off Miss Cambridge."

"Why is that?"

"I rather prefer more mature ladies," he explained, then a self-deprecating look settled on his face. "And besides, I've looked in a mirror more than once. There's not a chance that a beautiful girl like Miss Cambridge would ever look at me once, let alone twice."

"Did you perhaps get the impression that

Captain Gower was involved with Miss Cambridge himself?"

"That would seem jolly silly given he said she was dangerous and the insinuation that she had something to do with her husband's death was clear. Yet it seems the likely explanation for his heightened emotions."

Either that, or he was unhinged, as the other man had just suggested. It seemed everyone was keen for Tommy to believe that Ralph's behaviour was because of a mental imbalance. Everyone except for the groom, and although he had seemed an honest fellow, could he really be more informed than the staff that worked alongside Ralph every day? He knew he needed to take more notice of what most of the staff were saying and less of his own personal recollections of his old friend.

"Had he ever said anything like that to you before?"

"Never." The teacher shook his head firmly. "He had always seemed a rather level-headed and likeable fellow. I really couldn't tell you why his behaviour seemed so changed yesterday."

"Thank you for your time."

The maths master shook Tommy's hand enthusiastically. "You're welcome. Please don't hesitate to seek me out if there's anything else you think I can do to help."

Tommy thanked the other man. He couldn't

imagine that there was anything else he could do—he seemed as perplexed by Ralph's behaviour as everyone else at the school. He hoped Evelyn had made a breakthrough, as he didn't think they were any closer to finding Ralph's killer or cracking the code he'd left. Everything pointed to poor Ralph suffering a disturbance of the mind. Was it possible that the code meant absolutely nothing, and was simply part of Ralph's deteriorating mental state?

He didn't know, but he was even more determined to find out.

6

Edwin Miller, surprisingly, was in the school chapel. The small building was behind the main school building, and the classrooms, at the very edge of the property near the stables. The Davenport family had clearly used it for generations, which was evidenced by the tombstones that dotted the overgrown grass surrounding the chapel. Feeling like the worst kind of snooper, Evelyn edged forward to look at the newest headstone. It commemorated the life of Julia Davenport's mother and a couple of her brothers that had not lived past infancy. Her heart broke for the headmistress and her father. Losing a child was surely the very worst of nature. She shivered and suddenly couldn't wait to solve this murder and get back to Hessleham Hall where she could cuddle Isabelle and thank God for the blessings He had sent her way.

Evelyn hovered on the outside of the holy building—she didn't want to disturb Edwin Miller's quiet time, but she didn't want to miss him and have to spend another half an hour looking for him. Fortunately, the groom, Frank Mitchell, had spotted the senior master heading towards the chapel and given Evelyn a description of both the chapel and Mr Miller himself.

The man seemed to realise there was someone else nearby as he turned abruptly from where he was sitting on the pew at the front of the building. "Good morning."

"I'm terribly sorry to disturb you," Evelyn said. "I wonder if I might join you for a few minutes?"

"Of course, young lady. Do come in and join me." He patted the cushioned bench to his right as he shuffled along to make room for her.

"You are Edwin Miller?"

"I am," he said, a genial smile causing his eyes to crinkle at the edges and deep wrinkles to imprint themselves on either side of his mouth. "You have me at somewhat of a disadvantage. I'm afraid I don't know who you are."

"How rude of me." Evelyn returned his smile. "I am Evelyn Christie. I'm here at Docere House to enrol my daughter at the school."

Edwin Miller wagged a finger in Evelyn's direction. "Now, Lady Northmoor. You should introduce yourself properly."

Evelyn flushed. "It seems a little pretentious to introduce oneself as Lady Northmoor, when I am genuinely here as a parent and this is not a social occasion."

"I knew you and your husband were coming here today. I think everyone did. Miss Davenport is extremely excited that you and your husband have chosen Docere House."

"We never had another school in mind," Evelyn confided. "Lord Northmoor and his brother and sisters all attended Docere House. There was no question that our child would also come here. The only thing we did discuss was whether our child would board."

"And you decided your little darling should not?" he asked with a bewitching twinkle in his eyes.

Evelyn smiled in genuine amusement. "You are correct in your assumption. I was not keen for Isabelle to board when she starts. My husband and I have agreed that if Isabelle should wish to board when she is older, we will discuss the issue again then. Until such time, she will be brought to and from school each day by our driver."

"You seem a thoroughly modern young woman." The teacher nodded approvingly.

Evelyn reminded herself of the reason she was there to speak to Edwin Miller. Though she had sniffed delicately several times, she could detect the smell of alcohol on the man's breath. Of course, that wasn't the kind of question she could simply ask. She would have to discern for herself whether or not he was the sort of person who resorted to one drink too many. "That's a very polite way to put it. Unconventional is another word I hear a lot about myself."

"There's nothing wrong with allowing oneself to adjust along with the times," he said, looking towards the wooden cross on the wall in front of them. "In fact, it seems the most sensible of decisions."

"You sound as though you're here to make an important decision yourself," Evelyn said.

He nodded. "Miss Davenport told us that you and Lord Northmoor enjoyed asking questions—particularly when there was a mystery that you wanted to solve. Are you looking at the death of poor Mr Gower as something more nefarious?"

"I'm extremely sorry to say that we are," Evelyn confirmed. "It appears that Captain Gower's death was not natural."

"I'm very sorry to hear that."

"Are you?" she asked. "I rather understood that the two of you were not on friendly terms."

"Ralph was a pleasant fellow." Edwin nodded as he spoke, as though authenticating his own words. "Despite what happened, I liked him."

"What happened?" Evelyn feigned innocence. She didn't want to let the teacher know that Julia

Davenport had told her that Ralph had reported him.

"He told Miss Davenport that I was drinking." Edwin Miller looked away from Evelyn, as though deeply embarrassed by the confession. "I understand why he did that. He gave me several chances to tell the truth, but I'm afraid I did not."

"You were not drinking excessively and keeping alcohol in your classroom?" Evelyn asked.

"I was not," he said. "I *am not*."

"But you can understand why Captain Gower thought you were."

"Of course." Edwin Miller looked back at Evelyn. "And I shall tell you."

"I do believe it will be helpful if you do," she said, almost holding her breath as she waited for his explanation.

"I have Parkinsons," he said in a voice that was full of pain. "I received the diagnosis approximately three years ago. I have managed to hide the worst of the symptoms until very recently. A couple of the older boys realised I have a tremor. Of course, they put it down to excessive alcohol. Children of that age like to talk. Before long, every class I taught was full of pupils waiting to see me stumble, or drop something, or fail to recall the most simple of facts. Every time something like that happened, they had more evidence of my drinking. Or so they believed."

Evelyn reached forward and put a hand on the

liver-spotted one of Edwin Miller. "I'm so very sorry."

He placed his other hand on top of hers. She couldn't help but notice how obviously it shook as he did so. "You're very kind."

"You didn't tell Captain Gower about your diagnosis."

"I have told no one," he said. "That's partly why I am here now. I'm seeking some sort of guidance. I'm waiting for a sign."

"My husband was never much for attending church," Evelyn said. "Now he attends regularly. He has come to welcome the peace of a consecrated building, the benefits of prayer, and the understanding of God's will and His own timing."

The teacher chuckled. "You make your husband sound an impatient man. Which I sympathise with. I've asked God several times if it was time for me to retire. I accept that I am one of those people who rather expects an immediate answer."

"Which almost never happens."

"It does not." He patted Evelyn's hand and then folded his hands together on his lap. "However, with what has happened today, I think now is the time for me to be honest and accept that my time here at Docere House should come to a close."

"You've been here a long time?"

"Forty-four years." His eyes moistened and to Evelyn's horror, she thought the older man was going to cry. However, he drew in a deep breath and seemed to take control of his emotions. "I should have told Gower and Miss Davenport when they expressed their concerns for me, but I am afraid I was prideful. I didn't want to accept either the diagnosis or the effect that it would have on me."

"What is it about Captain Gower's death that makes you think now is the time to retire?" Evelyn fervently hoped he was not about to admit to killing Ralph in a fit of temper, as she rather liked the older man.

He lifted a shoulder as though in resignation. "He was cut down in his prime. That sort of thing makes one think about one's own mortality."

"Do you have any idea what may have happened to him?"

"I don't. I only wish I did. As I said to you earlier, although he reported his concerns to Miss Davenport about me, I liked him." His lips twisted in a ghost of a smile. "He did the right thing. My teaching has been substandard for a long time. He asked me for an explanation and I did not give one. He gave me several chances before he went to the headmistress. I can understand why he thought I was drinking. The older pupils here, I am afraid, are apt to believe that their perceptions of reality are fact."

"Can you think of anyone who had reason to be angry with Captain Gower?"

"Other than myself?" he shook his head as Evelyn was ready to interrupt. "No, my dear. I have a reason, as we both well know. However, I did not kill the man. I can give you the name of one other person who I know disliked Gower passionately. In fact, only this morning the rotter was rejoicing in his demise."

"Who is that?"

"Gilbert Wellesley." He held up a hand. "Now, before you dismiss this young man from your list of suspects, let me tell you that Gilbert Wellesley is an extremely spoiled youth. He has always had everything that he could possibly want, and yet instead of that making him a contented and happy individual, it has turned him into an overindulged, selfish, and quite unlikeable person."

"Why do you see him as a suspect?"

"I should have said." Edwin Miller's face turned serious. "I overheard him talking to his chums about Gower's death before class, had to tell him several times during our lesson to stop talking, and in the end threatened to send him to the headmistress if he did not concentrate on his work. The reason for his merriment was that Gower's death means he can no longer report Wellesley for cheating in a recent examination."

"He would want to avoid that at all costs?" Evelyn asked, a doubtful note in her voice. "Even commit murder to prevent Miss Davenport from finding out?"

"Oh, it wasn't the headmistress he was afraid of," Mr Miller said. "It was his parents. His father specifically. He's a government minister. The scandal could well affect his career detrimentally. Young Wellesley would do anything to avoid his father's wrath."

Evelyn got to her feet. "Thank you so much for speaking with me. I do hope you find answers to your questions very soon."

"Thank you, my dear."

"Good afternoon, Lord Northmoor." The imperious voice of Hessleham Hall's butler came through the telephone line. "How may I help you?"

"I wonder if either Miss Constance or Miss Grace are available to come to the telephone?"

"I'm afraid not, my lord. The young ladies have gone out with Lady Victoria. Something about a veil for the wedding, but I can't recall the exact detail."

Tommy didn't blame the butler. He didn't listen too carefully when either of his sisters or his Aunt Victoria spoke about the many accoutrements that Constance deemed necessary for her wedding to her fiancé Alexander Ryder, the 10th Earl of Chesden, in just a few months' time. "Oh dear. I wanted to ask them a question about their schooldays."

"Might Lady Emily be of assistance?" The butler's tone indicated that he very much hoped she might be. "She is standing right here at my elbow."

Tommy did not hide the smile that creased his face as he stood in the old drawing room, the room that had been assigned to the police, looking out of the window and desperately wishing the answer to Ralph's code would appear as if by magic into his mind. "I'm afraid not."

"Malton, I demand that you give me that instrument!" Aunt Em's voice came clearly over the line, as though she was engaged in wrestling the telephone receiver away from the butler. Which, knowing his great aunt as he did, was entirely possible. "Immediately!"

"Hello?"

"Tommy?"

"Aunt Em, how..."

"Never mind all that. Has there been a murder?"

"How can you possibly know that?" Even allowing for gossip in small villages, and households such as Hessleham Hall, he was surprised the news had travelled quite so quickly.

"Does that matter? Answer the question, my boy."

"I'm afraid so, Aunt Em."

"And the victim?" Her voice lowered in timbre,

the impatience replaced with sadness. "Was it your friend? The one you were hoping to see?"

"Yes, Aunt Em. It was. That is to say...it is. The victim is Ralph Gower."

"Have you found the vile perpetrator?"

Tommy had to smile at his aunt's faith in him and his investigative prowess. "Not yet."

"Then I shall get the butcher's boy to bring the car round immediately. He can drive me to Docere House, where I shall help you solve the mystery."

"Aunt Em, you know Albert hasn't been the butcher's boy for some time now. He's married to Nora; they have a child of their own, he's quite grown up."

"Yes, yes," his aunt said, and Tommy could imagine her waving a hand dismissively as though those things were of no consequence. "I know all that, but he'll always be the butcher's boy to me. Now if I ask Malton to fetch him immediately, I can be on my way.

He knew trying to divert Aunt Em was like trying to stop a runaway horse, but he tried anyway. "When are the girls due home? I have something I'd like to ask them."

"Does your question concern the murder?"

"Yes, it does."

"Then it's settled," Aunt Em said firmly. "The girls are due home before luncheon. As soon as we have dined, we shall be on our way."

Tommy swallowed. "All of you?"

"Well, no," Em said. "I shouldn't think Victoria will come with us. She's much too busy with wedding arrangements."

The relationship between Helen, their mother, and the four Christie siblings had been damaged severely owing to her behaviour immediately prior to her aborted wedding to the Marquis of York the previous summer. Aunt Victoria had stepped into the breach admirably and had quite taken over the organisation of Constance's wedding to Alexander Ryder. Which was no mean feat considering the wedding was to take place before Christmas that very year and at the Earl's country residence in County Wicklow, Ireland. Letters and telephone calls to the earl's residence in Ireland, Killeven Castle, seemed to occur daily. Tommy found himself worn out just thinking of the logistics Aunt Victoria was navigating in her usual steadfast and completely unflappable manner.

"I suppose the more of us that work on the code Ralph left, the sooner we will crack it."

"What is that?" Aunt Em asked sharply. "A code?"

"It's like a riddle, Aunt Em. He left a clue for me in his Bible. It just seems to me like it's a random jumble of letters and numbers, but I suppose it must mean something."

"Hmm," his aunt replied. "Rather like the Bible

itself. Much of that seems like a riddle to me. Either the words don't mean exactly what you think they should, or they are an allegory, or somehow symbolic rather than their meaning being clear and simple."

"Yes, I suppose," he agreed—something about Aunt Em's words was playing on his mind, but he couldn't quite grasp the thought. "Though quite often words mean exactly what you think they do."

"We'll see you directly after luncheon." He heard a muffled sound as his aunt passed the telephone to Malton. "Please tell cook that we shall eat as soon as the girls return home."

"Yes, my lady." Malton's voice seemed to come from far away. So much so, that Tommy almost jumped out of his skin when he spoke directly into the mouthpiece. "Are you still there, my lord?"

"Yes, Malton."

"Was there anything else?"

His aunt was on her way to Docere House, bringing with her a charm all of her own. He couldn't think of anything else he could possibly want. Except there was one more thing he should do before he put down the telephone. If he did not, Evelyn would never forgive him. "Is Lady Isabelle alright?"

"Oh yes, my lord," the butler replied immediately, his voice lifting in pure happiness. "I had call to be on the nursery floor quite recently. Lady

Isabelle is having a wonderful time with nanny and her cousin Miss Josephine."

Tommy could not think of a single reason for Malton's duties to take him anywhere near the nursery, but he saw no reason to mention that fact to the butler. "Wonderful, thank you so much. Lady Northmoor will be pleased."

As, of course, was he.

"Should you be wandering around the grounds unchaperoned?" The whiny voice demanded.

"Gilbert Wellesley?" Evelyn demanded in her best imitation of Aunt Em's haughtiest intonation.

"Flattered you know who I am, ma'am," he drawled in what Evelyn believed was Gilbert's emulation of American.

"I'm not here to listen to any of your nonsense," Evelyn snapped. "I understand you have been gloating about the death of Captain Gower."

The boy raised a shoulder in a gesture of pure insolence. "Who?"

"Mr Gower," Evelyn said with exaggerated patience. "Your science master."

"Oh, him." Gilbert looked at his fingernails.

"I imagine the letter he sent to your father before his death will make interesting reading."

Evelyn was gratified that her statement captured the student's attention. His gaze snapped to hers. "What?"

All colour had left the youth's face, and for a moment Evelyn felt almost guilty for her falsehood. "He caught you cheating. Your father won't be happy to read about that, will he?"

"He wouldn't!" Gilbert spluttered. "He wouldn't have done that! He said he would give me a chance to reform."

"Is that so?" Evelyn raised an eyebrow. "Yet you saw fit to revel in his untimely demise."

"I think perhaps you are mistaken," he said sulkily. "You have me mixed up with some of my more *childish* chums."

Evelyn was not about to let the upper sixth pupil off lightly. "No, I have it on very good authority that the person responsible is you."

"Good authority?" The boy guffawed, forgetting he was currently attempting to play the part of an injured party. "Do you mean old blotto face himself, Miller?"

"If you cannot speak about your masters with respect, I shall report you to Miss Davenport myself." Evelyn pinned the boy with her most severe glare. "Do you understand?"

"Yes..." the boy's bravado faltered as he cast about for a suitable way to refer to Evelyn. "Miss."

"I am Lady Northmoor," Evelyn said, pushing

home her advantage as the boy realised the time for playing silly games was most definitely up. "The daughter of Horace Hamilton. I believe your father knows my father, given they were both serving MPs at the same time."

Gilbert's Adam's apple bobbed painfully as he struggled to swallow. "Lady Northmoor. Gosh. I'm sorry. I didn't realise. Please..."

Evelyn held up a hand. "Stop wittering. It's embarrassing."

Gilbert hung his head. "Yes, my lady."

"Now, about your science master, Captain Gower. Have you any idea what happened to him?"

"He was a little green around the gills yesterday," Gilbert said. "Then next thing we know, the doctor is here, and someone said he'd died. Awful tragedy."

Evelyn ignored the fact the pupil had seemed quite happy that Ralph was dead until he knew who she was. "What do you know about that?"

"Me?" he squeaked. "Nothing."

"You certainly had something to gain from his death, though, didn't you?"

"Not if he'd already sent a letter to my father," Gilbert said, some of his earlier impertinence returning.

"But you didn't know he'd done that until I just told you he had." Evelyn pointed out. "So as far as I see it, you still had a motive to want him dead."

"Lady Northmoor." Gilbert drew himself up to his full height, doubtless in an attempt to make himself look as important as he thought he was. "I would not kill a fellow just to keep him quiet about a little misunderstanding over a science examination."

"Cheating," Evelyn said firmly. "You were caught cheating. There was no misunderstanding."

"Even so," he said, somewhat weakly, "I wouldn't ever hurt someone just to keep them quiet."

"Despite the quite terrible scandal it would cause if the newspapers got hold of the story?" Evelyn asked. "Your father's career could be seriously affected by such an article."

"I know." Gilbert poked the toe of one shiny shoe into the grass. "Papa would probably send me into the army immediately. Either that or something just as drastic."

"I suppose it would affect your chances of getting into a good university terribly," Evelyn suggested.

"Awfully," Gilbert agreed.

"You'd better tell me everything you know," Evelyn said. "And then, if I'm satisfied with what you have told me, I will do what I can to stop your father from ever receiving that letter."

"Can you?" he begged. "Can you really do that?"

"Of course," she replied with an air of superiority. "I can do almost anything I want. However, I would need to want to help you in that way. Do you understand, Gilbert?"

"Oh yes, Lady Northmoor." He nodded eagerly. "Yes, I do. I promise I will help you in any way that I can and I'll be certain to tell the other boys to lay off their jesting about Gower's death."

"And also the quite dreadful way you have treated Mr Miller," Evelyn said. "There will be no more talk about him being sozzled. You are quite wrong about him."

"Yes, Lady Northmoor," Gilbert said as meekly as a young child.

"Now, what can you tell me about Captain Gower? What have you seen or heard that may help?"

"Mr Adams detested him. He wanted his job. He was always bringing Gower coffee as though he was the world's best assistant, but we all knew he couldn't wait for Gower to mess up so he could take his job." The words practically ran together, Gilbert was in such a rush to get them out of his mouth.

"Surely it was kind of Mr Adams to bring his colleague coffee?"

"Not if he laced it with poison."

"Goodness, Gilbert, what on earth makes you think he did something like that?"

"Well, he is dead, isn't he?"

Evelyn couldn't argue with that logic, but she

needed a little more than the boy's fertile imagination. "Did you see him do anything like that?"

Gilbert shook his head. "No. But that doesn't mean he didn't, does it?"

"What did you see?"

The boy sighed. "Nothing. I wish I had. Imagine knowing who the murderer was. I'd be quite the hero then, wouldn't I?"

Instead of just a boy who had been caught cheating.

"Please think carefully about the last few days. If anything should come to your mind about Captain Gower, or someone acting suspiciously around him or his classroom, I'd be extremely grateful if you would tell me."

"What about my father and that dratted letter?"

"I shall speak to Lord Northmoor about it," Evelyn said. "You haven't told me anything useful yet and my husband and Captain Gower were *extremely* good chums during the war."

"Yes, I see." Gilbert looked as though the entire world rested on his shoulders, then the doom suddenly left him. "I'm sure between my pals and me we can find out something that will help. Someone must know something! May I be excused, my lady?"

Evelyn nodded and watched as Gilbert ran across the lawn away from her. While she hoped he would find out some much-needed information about Ralph Gower's last few days, she knew also that she had sent the boy off snooping for answers. With a murderer on the loose, it had the potential to be very dangerous.

A bell announcing lunch sounded and Evelyn hurried towards the main school building. Miss Davenport had sent word that a meal would be provided for them, together with the police, in the drawing room. No doubt Detective Inspector Andrews would expect a full account of everything they had found out so far. If so, he would be sorely disappointed. Evelyn didn't think she had learned a single thing of value—she could only hope Tommy had had more joy.

7

"Start from the beginning," Aunt Em demanded.

"We've just recapped everything we know for the police," Tommy groaned. "Do we really have to do it all over again?"

"I should think you do," Em retorted. "Especially since you've asked for our help."

That wasn't exactly how Tommy remembered their telephone conversation, but he knew his great aunt well enough not to argue the point with her. "As you know, shortly after our arrival, we found Ralph Gower dead in his bed."

"There was a book and a sheet of paper on top of his bedspread," Evelyn said. "He had started to write a letter to Tommy before he died. There was an ink stain where he had dropped his pen when he lost consciousness and an open Bible next to it."

"What did the letter say?" Aunt Em asked.

"He said he needed to tell me something," Tommy said. "But sadly, he did not finish the letter."

"On the telephone, you said something about a code. Grace reads lots of detective fiction. Tell her about it."

Tommy's younger sister flushed—whether in embarrassment at being singled out or perhaps with a sort of pride that Aunt Em thought she might be able to help, he wasn't sure. "As Evelyn said, the Bible was open next to Ralph. He had underlined a single word. That word was riddle."

"Which Bible was it?" Grace asked timidly, almost as though she were afraid to voice her opinion.

"Does that matter?"

She cleared her throat. "Well, yes, it might. If the code has something to do with the Bible, then the version Ralph was reading could be crucial."

"What makes you think the code has something to do with the Bible?"

"I'm just thinking out loud, Tommy. You mentioned the Bible, and that there was a word underlined in it. Carry on, tell us more."

"We then thought that perhaps Ralph's death might be suspicious. We had been told that his behaviour was unusual recently and his illness progressed rather quickly, so we wondered if it was possible that he had been poisoned. If there wasn't something odd about his illness, why would he underline one word in his Bible while writing to Tommy?"

"What do the police think?" Constance asked, ever a voice of reason.

"They were inclined to think it was just a tragic case of gastroenteritis," Tommy said to his elder sister. "That is, at first. Now they have listened to everything we have told them, they agree it is a murder, and we are facing a race against time to find the perpetrator before they either destroy all evidence or run away."

"Running away would rather signify their guilt," Aunt Em said. "That would be a spectacularly foolish thing for them to do."

"Indeed," Tommy agreed. "However, as we all know, murderers rarely think logically or too far in advance."

"We knew we might be jumping to conclusions," Evelyn said. "So we decided to search Captain Gower's private living quarters. In the living room, we found a book on a shelf. That, of course, wasn't unusual, but that particular volume was sticking out slightly. The other books were all neatly lined up."

"Was the book another clue?" Grace asked excitedly.

"Indeed it was," Tommy replied. "As I picked the

book up, Ralph's army service record card fell out. He had written on it that he was transferred to Intelligence Room 40."

"Oh, my goodness," Grace breathed. "He was a code breaker."

"How on earth do you know that?" Constance asked her sister.

"Because I spend more time reading books than shopping for clothes or looking at periodicals showing the latest hairstyles and whatnot."

Tommy stepped in before his sisters could debate the issue further. He knew his elder sister thought Grace should spend more time doing the things she herself did so she could find herself a beau—rather than spend her time in the library at Hessleham Hall reading about someone else's life. "In the margins of the book, Ralph had written some letters and numbers. I'm afraid they all seem like rather a jumble to me."

He extracted the paper from his pocket and laid it on the table in front of them so they could all see it.

"Where's the poetry book now?" Grace wondered.

"We put it back on the shelf for the police to find," Evelyn said.

"Did you tell them what you found?" Constance raised an eyebrow. "You really should have done, you know. You shouldn't hide things from the police."

"We didn't at first," Tommy admitted. "We left the book for them to find and decided if they weren't clever enough to see the word 'riddle' underlined in the Bible and look for further clues themselves, then we would not help them. However, we did tell them over lunch what we had found, and what we learned from the people we spoke to."

Grace sighed deeply. "You're right. It does just look like a complete muddle of letters and numbers."

"And yet it must mean something," Tommy said, frustration in each word.

"The word riddle being underlined is the first clue really, isn't it?" Grace asked. "Isn't the verse something about there being a riddle and thirty pieces of silver will be awarded if it's solved?"

"Yes, I think it's something like that." Evelyn got to her feet. "Why don't I get a Bible from the library? There's sure to be one in there and we'll have a look."

Tommy held up a hand. "Let's all go together. It would feel safer if we do that."

"What about all the suspects?" Aunt Em got slowly to her feet. "You haven't even told us about them and that's always my favourite part of your investigations."

"We will, Aunt Em, we will," Tommy reassured her.

As they opened the door to the drawing room and stepped out into the wide corridor, Nanny Bunting walked towards them. "Ah, there you are. I wondered if perhaps you were ready to complete your application for Lady Isabelle? Miss Davenport is otherwise engaged and asked if I could find you."

"Of course...ummm..."

"Nanny Bunting," the secretary said firmly. "It may seem rather odd to you to refer to me that way, Lady Northmoor. But it's what everyone calls me."

Tommy gave his wife one of their 'speaking looks'. He didn't particularly want Evelyn going anywhere he couldn't see her, but what harm could she possibly come to, going to the school office with the Davenports' old nanny?

"Let's take care of the application now," Evelyn said smoothly.

"Thank you, Lady Northmoor." Nanny Bunting looked at Tommy. "I shall bring Lady Northmoor to join you as soon as we are finished. Where shall we find you?"

"In the library," Tommy answered. "My younger sister Grace loves libraries, and I promised to show her yours. I hope you don't mind?"

"Why would we mind?" Nanny Bunting frowned. "What an odd thing to say, Lord Northmoor. It's just a library full of old books."

"Of course." He took Aunt Em's arm and they, together with Constance and Grace, headed right out of the drawing room as Evelyn and Nanny Bunting went left towards the entrance of the school and the secretary's office.

"Shall I send for tea?" Nanny Bunting asked.

Evelyn rested a hand on her stomach. "Oh goodness me, no. You served a wonderful lunch, which I have already washed down with what feels like a gallon of tea."

"Very well." She pushed a couple of sheets of paper, held together by a paperclip, towards Evelyn. "Perhaps you could fill this application form in for me?"

Evelyn picked up the pen the secretary offered and stared at the sheets in front of her. It was a very simple form. Her hesitation wasn't because she was wondering what she should write, but more because she was trying to remember what questions she and Tommy wanted to ask Nanny Bunting.

She completed a couple of lines and then looked up. "So sad about Captain Gower, isn't it? Did you know him very well?"

Nanny Bunting folder her arms across her ample bosom and leaned forward, resting her forearms on the desk. "He was a decent fellow."

Evelyn tried not to show her disappointment. She had been hoping for a little more than that as a conversation starter. "I'm pleased to hear you say so. Lord Northmoor has been most vexed to find that there are a number of people here at the school that seemed to dislike him."

"Really?" Despite one eyebrow raised in query, Nanny Bunting didn't sound in the least bit interested. "He always appeared all right to me."

"I assume that as the school secretary, it is your responsibility to send out requests for references for school staff?"

Nanny Bunting reached over and tapped the application form with a pen. "You must know I can't discuss things like that with you, Lady Northmoor. The form, if you please."

Evelyn bit her lip. "Of course."

She wrote for a couple of more minutes, all the while desperately trying to find a way into the secretary's confidence. If Daisy had overheard the argument between Ralph and the headmistress, as well as the curious mention of 'national security', then there was no way Nanny Bunting would not have heard it too.

"It's no good, Lady Northmoor," the secretary said, a touch of amusement in her voice. "It does not matter what you ask me, how you ask me it, or in how many ways, I shall not breach Miss Davenport's trust. Not simply because I am her employee, but because I have known her since she was a child. The Davenports are very important to me."

"I didn't—"

"No, you didn't say anything," Nanny Bunting agreed. "But I could practically hear the cogs inside your brain whirring away."

Evelyn, who prided herself on being able to talk to anyone, and receive whatever information she desired, was more than a little disconcerted to discover that this formidable woman seemed determined to thwart her every attempt to discover even the smallest piece of information.

"It may have escaped your attention, but someone has lost their life. A good man is dead. You really should think twice about who you trust and do whatever you can to help us uncover Captain Gower's killer," Evelyn said haughtily with her best impression of Aunt Em.

"Lady Northmoor, while it's jolly sad the man is dead, there's nothing I can do about it. I am just a secretary." She stared at Evelyn with a blank expression. "However, if I knew anything, I would certainly share that information with the police."

Evelyn was filled with a certainty that the woman knew something. She was Julia Davenport's secretary, so she would see and hear everything that went on in the school. She changed her tactics, making her voice low and full of sadness. "Lord Northmoor was desperately sad to hear about Miss Cambridge's husband. Too many young soldiers came home from war and could not adjust to life as a civilian."

"Indeed," the secretary murmured. "But then Miss Cambridge's husband was hardly a young man."

"Oh really?" Evelyn asked, jumping on the secretary's words, and hoping she would say more.

Nanny Bunting pulled a face. "You shall get no more from me. I've said enough."

Yet she'd barely said anything. Could it be possible that the one thing she had said was important? Evelyn couldn't believe that it was, yet she resolved to find out more. She couldn't imagine that Clarissa Cambridge's husband could have anything to do with Ralph's death. The only link she could see between the two men was that they had both been soldiers. Was it possible Clarissa knew something about Ralph from her husband?

This investigation was making her head hurt. She fervently hoped that Tommy, Aunt Em, and the girls had found out something new in the library because she feared she was drawing a complete blank from her time with Nanny Bunting.

Looking down at the paper in front of her, Evelyn continued to fill out the form in her small, neat handwriting, while the secretary looked on with a look on her face that was very slightly gleeful.

Tommy was glad when Nanny Bunting brought Evelyn back to them, as promised.

"Is there anything I can get for you, my lord?"

"No, thank you. We will sit in here and catch up for a while, if that is all right."

"Of course, Lord Northmoor." The secretary paused at the door. "Shall I close the door?"

"If you wouldn't mind, that would be splendid." He waited until she had done so and turned to Evelyn. "Well?"

"I'm afraid I didn't find out a single thing," she said. "Nanny Bunting is the sort of tight-lipped faithful employee everyone wishes they had."

"How boring," Aunt Em commented.

"Dreadfully," Evelyn agreed. "The only thing she did say that was possibly of any interest was that Miss Cambridge's husband was much older than her."

"How is that relevant?" Tommy wondered.

"I can't imagine," Evelyn said. "And yet because it was the only thing she said, I can't help but feel it must mean something."

"Should I telephone to my contact?" Aunt Em asked with a wicked twinkle in her pale blue eyes.

"Your contact, Aunt?"

"You know, my boy," Em said impatiently. "The one who gets the information we need from Somerset House."

"I don't suppose it can hurt," he said with little enthusiasm. What could it matter who her husband had been?

"Aunt Em is right. We should find out who Miss Cambridge was married to," Evelyn said. "It's possible he knew Ralph."

"Simply because they were both in the army?" Tommy asked. "Tens of thousands of men went to war."

"I know, but they both have a link to this area." Evelyn shrugged. "We should follow every lead."

"What other leads do you have?" Grace asked.

"None, just the code," Tommy said miserably.

"Who are the suspects?" Aunt Em asked eagerly.

"There's Bertie Adams." Tommy took a seat at the desk in the corner of the library that overlooked the grounds. He placed the piece of paper containing the codes they had found so far in front of him. "He is...was...Captain Gower's assistant."

"His motive is that he wants Ralph's job," Evelyn added.

"He told us that Ralph was conducting experiments in the laboratory alone. Miss Davenport was rather annoyed about this, too. Apparently, it's acceptable for the teachers here to use school equipment, but there's an expectation that if they do so, they share their findings with other members of staff—particularly junior ones."

"Bertie says that he asked the captain about his experiments, but he refused to even tell him what he was doing," Evelyn said. "He also stated that Ralph's behaviour had changed. Not only was he secretive about his work, but he seemed nervous that he was being followed, and had started to talk to himself."

Aunt Em shook her head. "How sad. Was he losing his mind?"

"I don't think so," Tommy said. "While we were in the classroom, I found a pile of berries on the windowsill. Underneath the berries was a note with more numbers and letters."

Evelyn pointed at the second code on the paper in front of Tommy. "These ones here."

"This one is the same," Grace said as she pointed at the last group in the first set, and the first group of numbers and letters in the second. "J3:12,9. It must be important if he used them twice."

"Carry on," Aunt Em urged as Grace stared at the paper as though willing the answer to jump out at her.

"I asked Bertie if he knew what the berries were." Tommy paused. "He said they were from a yew tree and the upshot is that they can be turned into something called a taxine, which is incredibly poisonous. He was very clear that the only person at the school who would know how to do such a thing was Ralph himself."

"And you think that was the secret experiment he was carrying out and, somehow, he was then poisoned by that very thing?" Em asked perceptively.

"Yes," Tommy said. "Ralph's symptoms and those that one would get from taxine poisoning are identical."

"I also spoke to the housemaid," Evelyn went on. "Daisy is a very sweet girl who told me that she overheard Captain Gower disagreeing with Miss Davenport where he said something along the lines of 'it was a matter of national security'."

"What was?" Grace asked, looking up.

"That's just the thing. She doesn't know."

"What did the headmistress have to say about it?" Aunt Em asked.

"I asked in a roundabout way," Evelyn said. "I didn't want to get Daisy into any trouble. So I asked about how the school asks for references for their staff. Then I suggested it was possible someone here had sympathies with England's enemies."

"Oh, Ev, you didn't!" Constance gasped in shock. "What did she say?"

"She was quite furious," Evelyn conceded. "But then she would be either way, wouldn't she? If there is someone like that here, she would act outraged so our suspicions wouldn't be raised, and if there isn't, then she'd rightly be extremely angry."

"Did she say anything else?" Constance asked.

"She reiterated that Ralph's behaviour had deteriorated recently," Tommy admitted. "That brings us to Clarissa Cambridge. She was the reason I telephoned to Hessleham Hall."

Constance's nose wrinkled. "I remember her. She was the year above me. Quite the swot. The teachers all loved her, the students did not."

"Oh?" Tommy raised an eyebrow as he looked at his sister with interest. "Why not?"

"She would tell tales about her own grandmother if she thought it would get her a better grade, or more well thought of by the teachers."

"Did she have any particular friends?"

"Goodness me, no." Constance laughed at the very thought. "None of the girls liked her. She left during the war, as I remember. Probably to marry that fellow that Evelyn said earlier was much older than her."

"How would she have met him?" Tommy asked. "I can't imagine the school allowing their young ladies to leave the premises to meet men."

"Oh, Tommy," Constance said fondly. "This isn't the Victorian era, you know. We were allowed to go to local dances and the like. Of course, we were usually very carefully chaperoned."

"Usually?"

"Things were a little more lax than normal during the war years, Tommy. The school didn't have the normal levels of staff."

"So it's possible she could have met her future husband at one of those not-very-well-chaperoned events?"

"I suppose so." Constance pulled a face. "Though it would be rather odd for a fellow much older than Clarissa to be at a dance for schoolgirls. Even if those girls were in the sixth form."

"It would," he agreed. "I'm sure if Father had known that sort of thing was going on, he would have removed you from school and brought you home immediately."

"Let's move on," Constance suggested. "Aunt Em can contact her person at Somerset House in case that helps. Who did you talk to next?"

Tommy blinked, as he always did when he remembered his sister was not a sixteen-year-old schoolgirl who needed careful watching and introduction to only the best young men. She was twenty-five years old and engaged to a man who, although Tommy hadn't liked him when they first met, was not only in a position to take care of Constance but also seemed to genuinely adore her.

"I spoke to Francis Galbraith, one of the maths masters. We had been told that he had an argument with Ralph only yesterday. He was at great pains to assure me that whilst Ralph was angry with him, he had no quarrel with Ralph. He told me Ralph said he would end up in the ground like Miss Cambridge's husband if he didn't stay away from her."

"Did they have an understanding?" Aunt Em asked.

"That's just the thing." Tommy pulled a hand through his hair in frustration. "No. He said he would never entertain ideas in her direction as she was jolly attractive, and he was a rather plain chap."

"He was another person we spoke to who commented on Captain Gower's altered mental state," Evelyn said quietly, as though reluctant to mention that particular issue once more. "Julia Davenport gave Edwin Miller's name to me as someone I may wish to speak to, as she knew there had been a disagreement between him and Captain Gower."

"Was there anyone the fellow hadn't had a dispute with before his demise?" Aunt Em wondered with her usual candidness.

Tommy sighed. "It appears that there's quite a list."

"Mr Miller had been accused by Captain Gower of being an alcoholic. He told me that Captain Gower gave him several chances to tell the truth about his situation, but he chose not to. Eventually, because the quality of his teaching was affected, he had to report the matter to Miss Davenport."

"Was Captain Gower's assumption incorrect?" Aunt Em asked.

"It was," Evelyn confirmed. "I will not say any more about Mr Miller other than he did have a motive to kill Captain Gower, but he assures me that he did not."

Tommy agreed with Evelyn's decision not to disclose the details of the teacher's illness. It wasn't for them to discuss what they had found out. If Mr Miller chose to make his diagnosis public, that was for him to decide. They had, of course, told the police, as he believed the detectives needed to know that information.

"Finally Evelyn spoke to one of the pupils. Ralph had caught him cheating and, because his father is a government minister, he is extremely keen to ensure no one finds out about his indiscretion."

"Is that really motive enough for murder?" Constance asked doubtfully.

"He is a rather unpleasant character," Evelyn said. "Though whether he would do something so drastic is unlikely, in my opinion."

Grace, who had been standing next to Tommy and looking over his shoulder at the paper containing the code, walked past him and over to the bookshelves. Not finding what she was looking for, she moved on to the next one.

"Here!" she exclaimed.

"Have you solved the riddle?" Aunt Em asked excitedly.

Grace turned, a thick book in her hands, a look of confusion on her face. "No, Aunt, I've found a King James Bible."

Aunt Em's look of great disappointment was almost comical. "Oh. Is that all?"

"As you have heard," Tommy said as he glanced around at his family, "we have lots of suspects, plenty of motives, but no real clue who it can be."

Grace put the Bible down on the desk and, as she did so, the single page containing the codes fluttered onto the floor. "Oh dear. I'm so sorry."

Tommy pushed back his chair. He got to his knees to retrieve the paper. As he grabbed it, he tried to get up too quickly and banged his head on the table. Reaching out a hand to rub his head, it brushed against something that was most definitely out of place on the underside of the desk.

"Tommy?"

"There's something here," he said, excitement in his voice. "I think it's another clue."

"Well, that's not much use to us if we can't crack the code, is it?" Aunt Em asked practically.

Tommy got back to his feet. "We'll do it, Aunt Em. Have some faith."

A moment earlier, he was feeling just as defeated as Aunt Em sounded. Now, finding this new clue, he felt invigorated and certain they would prevail.

"What does it say?" Grace asked eagerly as she flipped through the pages of the Bible.

The library door opened, and Tommy passed the scrap of paper he'd grabbed from under the desk to Grace as Bertie Adams walked into the room.

The code under the desk in the library read:

N13:16,12

G49:6,9

N20:21,7

8

There were many things he'd rather do—walking in the grounds of Docere House with Bertie Adams was most definitely not one of them.

"I really must insist on being allowed access to the library," the science master said in a sulky voice.

"What research do you want to carry out?" Tommy asked, not attempting to hide the suspicion in his voice.

"It's for a lesson I'm preparing," Bertie answered evasively.

"On what?" Tommy pressed.

"It's a specific scientific experiment,"

"Well." Tommy stopped walking and glanced back towards the library. The fact he could see the room did nothing for his impatience. He didn't want to be talking to Ralph's assistant. He did, however, want to be in the library looking at the new clue they had uncovered. "That is hardly surprising, given that you are a science master. I'd be shocked if you were researching the Sahara Desert, for instance."

"I don't have to tell you anything."

"No, you don't," Tommy agreed. "However, if you don't, it will seem to me as though you were hanging around the library because you wanted to find out what my family and I were discussing."

"But I wasn't."

"How can I believe what you're saying when you tell me you came to do research, but you won't tell me what that is?"

Bertie shuffled his feet nervously, then blurted out. "I wanted to see if I could find out how to make taxine."

"What on earth for?" Tommy demanded.

"Gower did it," he said. "I think I can too."

"All right," Tommy replied with exaggerated patience. "But why? Why would you want to do that when doing so could well have led to Captain Gower's death?"

"Well, if you must know, I rather admired him," Bertie said with great reluctance, as though Tommy had to physically drag the confession out of him.

"Did you indeed." Tommy looked at the other man, who had flushed a deep red and was looking off towards the long driveway of the school—

anywhere, in fact, but back at Tommy. "Why, then, were you so keen to get him into trouble with Miss Davenport?"

"Isn't that obvious?" He asked petulantly. "I was jealous. There. Now you have the truth. I was jealous of your precious friend. He was an absolute genius. I wanted to be just like him, and he wouldn't let me."

"Gosh," Tommy said, not expecting Bertie's outburst and almost at a loss to know how to respond. "I wasn't expecting you to say something like that."

"Well, there you have it." Bertie spread out his hands. "So you see, I had no reason to want him dead. I much preferred him to be alive so I could learn from him."

"You wanted his job," Tommy stated.

"No." He shook his head emphatically. "Not really. I wasn't ready for it. I know that."

"Who do you think killed him?"

"I don't know," Bertie said miserably. "I just know that it wasn't me."

"If anyone was going to slip some of the taxine into his food or drink, you were most handily placed to do so." Tommy faced Ralph's assistant and gave him his most piercing glare. "If what you've told me is right, that's how he was killed."

"We don't know that." Bertie backed away from Tommy. "All we know is that his symptoms are the same as taxine poisoning and he was working on something secretive. It could've been something completely unrelated."

"And yet you are so convinced that's what he was doing, you want to see if there are any books in the library that will teach you how to do the very same thing."

Bertie deflated in front of Tommy's eyes. "It wasn't me."

"If it wasn't you, who was it?" Tommy asked stonily. "We are talking about a man who served his country admirably and who has been cut down in the very prime of his life. If you know anything else, you need to share it with me immediately."

"I only wish I did, Lord Northmoor. I really do."

Although the science master's words had the ring of truth about them, Tommy wasn't completely convinced. It was more than possible that Bertie Adams's jealousy had led him to kill Ralph Gower out of pure spite. Despite the rather sorry state Bertie currently presented, Tommy wasn't yet ready to strike his name from the list of suspects.

"More letters and numbers," Constance said morosely.

"I think the riddle clue is from Judges." Grace flicked through the pages of the Bible with an ever-increasing urgency. "Ah, here it is. Chapter 14, verse 12."

"Say that again," Evelyn said, her sister-in-law's excitement rubbing off on her.

"Judges Chapter 14, verse 12?"

Evelyn grabbed the paper off the table, her hands shaking. "Read Judges 3, Chapter 12."

Grace found the right page and read. "'*And the children of Israel did evil again in the sight of the Lord—*'"

"Stop." Evelyn held up a hand. "*In*? That makes no sense."

"You're the one not making sense," Aunt Em retorted. "What are you talking about, Evelyn? What do you mean 'in', and why does it make no sense?"

"It's the ninth word in that chapter and verse." Evelyn put the paper back on the desk and pointed at the last code in the first group. Judges, Chapter 3, verse 12, the ninth word. The ninth word is 'in', but I don't see how that word would be part of a code."

"Judges isn't the only book in the Bible that begins with the letter J, though, is it?" Aunt Em's earlier scepticism had gone, and she now sounded as exhilarated as Evelyn and Grace.

"Let's start at the beginning," Constance suggested. "The first clue starts with the letter R. Turn to Ruth, Chapter 1, verse 29."

Irritation etched lines across Grace's face. "There isn't a verse 29."

"Romans," Aunt Em said. "Try Romans."

Grace flipped forward to the New Testament and found the right chapter and verse. "'Being filled with all unrighteousness, fornication, wickedness, covetousness, maliciousness; full of envy, murder—'"

"Oh my," Constance breathed. "The thirteenth word is murder."

"We've done it!" Aunt Em announced triumphantly. "This must be it, girls."

"Isaiah Chapter 41," Evelyn said.

Grace again found the right page, checked the verse, and counted out the words. "Tree."

"Now," Aunt Em said. "Joshua, Judith, Job, Jeremiah, Joel? Goodness, why are there so many books starting with a J?"

Nothing made any sense until they eventually searched through the New Testament and found the word berries hidden in the words of the Book of James.

"Murder, tree, berries," Evelyn said. "Ralph is telling us that he was murdered by the berries on the tree."

Within minutes, after rejecting words that didn't seem to fit, they had solved the second set of code.

"Berries, poison, books." Constance looked around. "He was pointing us to this room because this is where we found the third set of code. Of course, Tommy found it accidentally when Grace knocked the paper onto the floor, but Ralph was telling us this is where we need to be."

Grace gasped as they realised what the first word in the third set of code was. "Spy. Oh, Evelyn, is Ralph telling us there is a spy here in the school?"

Evelyn's lips thinned into a straight line. "That would make sense given he was overheard arguing with Julia Davenport about national security. He must have realised she had employed someone who was a risk to the safety of the country."

Constance shivered. "Ev, I confess, I'm a little afraid. I didn't think a visit to my old school would have me working out code in the library and realising there is a spy in our midst."

"Secret"—Grace called out—"passage. Secret passage! He must have left us more clues in a secret passage. Do you think he meant it's here in the library?"

Evelyn lifted a shoulder. "I don't know. Let's look."

"Come along, Constance." Aunt Em grabbed hold of her great-niece's hand and rubbed it. "Pull yourself together, my dear. We have work to do. Think of how proud Lord Chesden will be when you tell him you have been involved in catching a spy."

Constance still looked quite terrified but allowed a small smile to turn up her mouth at the corners. "Alexander *would* be proud."

"Catching a spy is much more impressive than having a new dress or a modern hairstyle." Grace grinned at her sister.

"If I find the secret passage before you, then you must write every one of my thank-you cards after the wedding."

Grace didn't pause. "You'll never do it!"

The girls hurried off to pull out books, tap floorboards and press any and every slight irregularity in the wood of the bookcases.

"Evelyn?" Aunt Em said quietly.

"Tommy will be devastated," Evelyn said with a quick glance out of the window. She could see her husband walking and talking with Bertie Adams, but desperately wished he was in the room with them. "We've both known for some time that poor Captain Gower was murdered, but this confirmation, and the fact that it seems likely he was killed by someone who is an enemy of England, will absolutely knock the stuffing out of him."

"Especially given the way he is about the war," Aunt Em said sympathetically. "That boy has already seen enough, coped with too much."

He refused to talk to her about the war, and Evelyn knew why. He didn't want to bring the brutal reality into their marriage. Although she desperately yearned to give him the comfort he often needed, she understood he would never share that with her.

"We simply must find the secret passage and Ralph's next clues."

Aunt Em nodded as her expression turned from grim to determined. "Yes, we must."

Aunt Em moved over to the large windows, peered at the windowsills outside, and ran her hands down the walls either side. Evelyn dropped to her knees and got busy rolling up the edge of the rug in the middle of the library floor.

Behind her, the library door was shoved open and something thrown onto the rug next to her. It took her a moment before she realised someone had thrown an old oil lamp into the room.

She got to her feet and staggered backwards as the unmistakable grating of a key being turned in the lock sounded.

Flames licked greedily at the rug and Evelyn stared at the other women in horror. "We've been locked in! We're trapped!"

9

Horror momentarily froze Tommy's feet to the grass on the lawn outside the library. He stared into the room. Aunt Em stood by the windows, Constance and Grace close behind her. From his vantage point, he couldn't see Evelyn, but he was as sure as he could be that she was trying to put out the fire or get the rest of his family out of the library safely.

Behind Aunt Em, flames rose like the fiery fingers of hell. Smoke swirled around the room. Should he find a rock, or other projectile, to throw through the window, or would that cause the fire to spread more quickly? He wished he knew the answer.

"There's a bucket of sand at the back of the house!" Bertie called. "You go inside, and I'll fetch the sand to put out the fire."

Tommy wasn't so sure. It looked as though it was taking a stronger hold with each passing second. It might take a whole beach to put out the blaze.

It seemed like forever before adrenalin coursed through him and galvanised him into action. He sprinted to the front of the house and threw open the heavy outer door. He was vaguely aware of shouting and a general sense of pandemonium as he ran along the corridor to the library.

Tommy grasped the doorknob and twisted it. Nothing happened. Using his shoulder, he shoved against the thick wooden door. The door was locked! He slammed on the door with the flat of his hands. "Evelyn!"

"Lord Northmoor? What is going on?" Detective Inspector Andrews hurried to join him, his colleague not far behind.

"There's a fire in the library," Tommy panted. "My wife, my aunt, and my sisters are inside. I think the door is locked!"

"All right." The detective held up a hand. "Let's not panic."

"Not panic?" Tommy shouted. "Did you not hear me, man? My family is in there!"

"Sir?" Detective Sergeant Montgomery stepped forward. "If you both move out of the way, I can try to break down the door."

The detective sergeant had the physique of a

rugby player. His shoulders were nearly as wide as the door itself. With great reluctance, Tommy stood back to give the larger man room to run at the door.

Detective Sergeant Montgomery's considerable frame hit the wood with a resounding thump. Although the door shook, it did not budge.

"Again!" Detective Inspector Andrews encouraged.

His junior gritted his teeth and ran at the door once more. This time, the door flew open with a loud crack of splintering wood. The rug in the centre of the room was well alight. Evelyn had an arm around Aunt Em as all four women hurried forward. They all held delicate, lacy handkerchiefs over the lower half of their faces. Bizarrely, he couldn't help but think it was about time a use had been found for those tiny scraps of material.

"Is everyone all right?" Detective Inspector Andrews asked.

Running feet sounded behind them as Bertie Adams, followed by other men, hurried along the corridor towards them. Each of them held a container of some sort. Bertie had a metal pail, others had kitchen pots. Another held a potted plant. They threw the contents of their receptacles onto the fire. Sand and soil landed on the rug and the fire diminished somewhat.

Coughing, and with their eyes streaming, Evelyn, Aunt Em, and the girls stood in the corridor outside the library. Constance and Grace clung to each other, their faces white with shock.

"What happened?" Tommy asked.

"Someone threw an oil lamp onto the rug," Evelyn said grimly. "Then locked the door so we couldn't escape."

"Someone deliberately tried to kill you?" Tommy asked, hating the faint note of doubt in his voice. Not that he didn't believe Evelyn. However, it was hard to accept that someone would take such risks when the police were in the building.

"I shouldn't have thought so," Evelyn answered in her usual matter-of-fact way. Already, she had regained most of her usual poise.

"I disagree." Aunt Em gave a delicate cough. "We were very nearly burned to death. What do you think the villain was trying to do? Provide us with a form of unnecessary heating?"

"Come along to the drawing room," the detective inspector said. "We need to talk, and I think it is best we do it in private."

"Shouldn't we stay to extinguish the fire?" Tommy asked.

"Montgomery can supervise that." Detective Inspector Andrews pointed down the corridor. "After you, ladies."

"Thank you." Tommy grasped the junior detective's hand in his. "From the very bottom of my heart, I thank you. I don't know what I'd have done if you hadn't broken down the door so swiftly."

"It was nothing, my lord." The other man flushed at Tommy's exuberant praise. "I'm sure you would have thought of something if I hadn't broken through."

"We'll never know that now, will we?" Tommy gave the man's hand one last hearty shake, wincing as his hand touched the other man's. It was possible he had the biggest splinter in history lodged in his palm. "I shall be forever in your debt."

Leaving the completely embarrassed detective helping put out the fire, Tommy hurried to join his family in the drawing room.

"I insist you stop investigating immediately," the detective inspector said before they had even had a chance to sit down.

"I don't agree." Evelyn sat on a high-backed chair and folded her hands in her lap.

"With respect—"

"I am calling for the car," Tommy said. "You must all return to Hessleham Hall immediately."

Evelyn glared at her husband, forgetting there was anyone else in the room but the two of them. "No."

"I'm sorry, Evelyn," he said. Even through her

anger, she could hear the genuine regret in his voice. "I rarely insist on anything, you know that. But on this occasion, I simply must."

"Unless you intend to pick me up and bodily remove me from Docere House, I'm not sure how you will get what you want," she replied tartly.

"I'm more than ready to leave," Aunt Em offered, looking between Tommy and Evelyn with concern. "The poor butcher's boy will have to turn around as soon as he reaches Hessleham Hall and come straight back to collect us."

"I could just arrest you." Detective Inspector Andrews stared at Evelyn with what she presumed was his most intimidating glare. It did not work on her.

"On what charge?"

"Interfering with an investigation, impeding a policeman in his duties, or tampering with evidence. Any of those. Take your pick."

Evelyn wasn't sure if any of the things he named were real offences. They all certainly sounded as though they could be. It didn't matter. The police officer's threats did not diminish her resolve. She held out her wrists towards him. "As you wish. Though I shouldn't like to be you when you explain to your chief superintendent how you arrested me shortly after I survived a quite horrific arson attack. I don't think that I have ever mentioned before now that his wife and I serve on several committees together."

"I went to school with the chief constable's daughter," Grace said timidly. "I'm sure she would simply hate to tell her father about the complete circumstances of Lady Northmoor's arrest."

"And I should simply hate to tell him," the detective began with clear sarcasm, "that I sought an agreement from both Lord and Lady Northmoor at the very beginning of this case about what would happen if the case became dangerous. Now that time has come, I am frustrated to hear that you refuse to make good on your promise, Lady Northmoor."

"I have an idea." Constance moved to stand next to Evelyn. "Would it inconvenience you awfully if we stayed in the library to wait for our chauffeur once the fire is out?"

"Why on earth would you want to do that?" The detective asked suspiciously, as though suspecting some kind of subterfuge, but couldn't work out what it could be.

"My sister loves to read," she said then leaned forward as though to share a confidence. "It will help her stay calm until our chauffeur arrives."

Grace walked over to her sister and stood on the other side of Evelyn's chair. "That's true, it will. And I should love to spend a little more time in the school's wonderful library."

Evelyn's heart felt as though it would burst right out of her chest. Although her sisters-in-law had been absolutely petrified when the library rug caught alight, they were both willing to stand by her side, both literally and figuratively. Not just that, but against their brother.

"It will take some time for the boy to arrive with the car," Aunt Em said imperiously. "Even if we telephone for him to come immediately. Perhaps if you post a police officer immediately outside the library door, and one outside in the grounds, we will be safe?"

The detective looked at the four women, then at Tommy. "Are they always like this?"

Tommy pulled a hand through his hair. "I'm afraid so. When the women of my family have made up their minds, it's quite impossible to for me to encourage them to alter it. We agreed to stop investigating if it got dangerous, not leave Docere House, so if the ladies want to spend some time in the library while they wait for the motor car, that should be acceptable, should it not?"

Evelyn let out a breath. Although she knew Tommy would, rightly, be furious with her for directly contradicting him in front of everyone, he had come down on her side. She really was very lucky to have such an understanding husband. Especially when he did not know why they were all so keen to spend more time in the library.

"Is that settled?" Grace asked.

"I suppose if I station a man outside the door, and in the grounds, as Lady Emily suggested, it will be all right." The detective inspector pierced Evelyn with a glare no more impressive, at least to her, than his earlier one. "No more investigating, Lady Northmoor."

"I wonder..." Constance said hesitatingly, before Evelyn could respond. "Would it be possible for us to spend a few moments catching up with Clarissa Cambridge? We were at school here together. I haven't seen her for simply ages."

"That would be fabulous," Grace simpered in a voice Evelyn had never heard her use before. "I do so love speaking with old friends. Wait until she hears who you're engaged to, Constance!"

Evelyn didn't think there could possibly be a single person in the entire land who was not aware that Constance was engaged to be married to Alexander Ryder, the 10th Earl of Chesden. Miss Cambridge might spend most of her time at Docere House, but surely she wasn't so far removed from society that she hadn't heard the news.

Detective Inspector Andrews didn't seem to think that Grace's artful suggestion was the least bit odd. His face creased into a friendly smile and he looked at the younger girl indulgently. "Of course, Miss Christie. I shall see to it myself that your friend joins you in the library. You ladies spend as much time as you like chatting and gossiping while you wait for your chauffeur."

The detective did not know that the meekest member of their family had outmanoeuvred him. Perhaps it was time that they all saw Grace as more than a timid little bookworm. She was a rather cunning young lady who, like the rest of their family, had a backbone made of the strongest steel.

"Can I leave the ladies in your safe care?" Tommy asked, walking towards the door.

"And where might you be going, Lord Northmoor?"

Tommy held up his hand. "I thought I would see if Nanny Bunting has something with which to take this splinter out of my hand and then dress it."

"Tommy!" Evelyn got to her feet and hurried over to him. "Why didn't you tell me you had injured yourself?"

"Rather embarrassing, actually," he said in a clear attempt to play down both the incident and the injury. "I banged on the library door. I think half of the wood is now stuck in my palm."

"Isn't that a little dramatic?" Aunt Em arched an eyebrow. "Especially for a former soldier."

"It's actually rather painful, Aunt," Tommy insisted. "It needs tending."

"I can just see the tiniest sliver of wood," Evelyn whispered.

"We can see that, darling, but Detective

Inspector Andrews cannot," Tommy answered. "I think a dressing is in order."

"It definitely needs tending to," Evelyn said in a louder voice.

The detective held up a hand. "Stay here, all of you. I will see if the library is safe for the ladies. We must hurry and catch whoever set the fire. The murderer is getting quite rash. Who knows what he'll do next?"

Tommy hurried out of the drawing room before Detective Inspector Andrews could ask to look at his hand. As he passed by the library, he was pleased that the fire had been completely extinguished.

"Is everyone all right?" Bertie Adams called.

Tommy couldn't fault the man. He hadn't liked him when he first met him, but Ralph's assistant had jumped into action quicker than Tommy himself had. "Yes, thank you. Your swift assistance is much appreciated."

"It was the least I could do." The teacher hung his head. "I only wish there was more I could have done to help Mr Gower instead of thinking of myself."

"I don't think there's anything you could have done differently," Tommy said honestly. "When someone has murder on their mind it's exceptionally difficult to stop it from taking place."

The other man nodded, his expression pensive, as Tommy carried on down the corridor towards Nanny Bunting's office.

Although Bertie Adams seemed to regret his earlier behaviour, and admitted it was because he was jealous of Ralph, he still couldn't be ruled out as a suspect. Of course, he couldn't have set the fire and locked the ladies in the library, but that didn't mean he wasn't working with the person who did.

Bertie had seemed so keen to get into the library —was it possible he was also working on the clues? Had he cracked the code and knew the next clue was in that room? They had also been told that Bertie regularly made coffee for Ralph.

Tommy's head whirled with the various possibilities. He always hated this time in an investigation where the end appeared to be near, yet simultaneously uncovering the perpetrator seemed impossible.

Surely, with police in and around the library, his family would be safe while he took a few minutes to speak with Julia Davenport's secretary. He didn't intend to be any longer than that. Who knew what fool idea Evelyn would come up with next so she could escape the confines of the room she'd promised to stay in and go off and interview someone else?

He had more or less ordered her to leave Docere House for her own safety and she had ignored him, stubbornly telling him that she would not leave. While he admired her bravery and resilience, he wished she would go home where it was safe. However, he was not foolish enough to suggest once more that is what she should do—when Evelyn had decided to do something, he knew better than most that it was very unlikely that her decision would change.

Nanny Bunting was typing away as he entered the room. Her grey hair was perfectly in place, as though each strand bended to her will and dare not disobey her. She must be a wonderful source of support to Miss Davenport.

"Ah, Lord Northmoor, how can I help you? Lady Northmoor completed the application form for Lady Isabelle earlier."

"Yes," Tommy said. "She told me. However, I'm afraid there's a problem."

She folded her hands on the desk in front of her, edging her typewriter slightly backwards as she did so. "I'm sorry to hear that. May I ask the nature of the problem?"

"We have decided that we no longer wish our daughter to attend school here."

"Oh no!" Nanny Bunting gasped in what seemed like genuine astonishment and sorrow. "Why have you changed your minds?"

"My friend has been murdered," Tommy said with feeling. "Then my wife, sisters, and aunt were imprisoned in your library and the rug set on fire. I do not feel that this is an appropriate place for Isabelle. If we are not safe when visiting, how could we hope our child would be while attending school?"

Nanny Bunting pursed her lips and Tommy could tell there was something she wanted to say, but dare not. "I see."

"I'm sure you think that we have angered someone by investigating Ralph's death." Tommy sat in the chair opposite the secretary. "While I am certain that these are very unusual times at Docere House, the fact remains that my friend has been killed and you have a killer on your staff."

"I don't see how you have jumped to that conclusion," she said stiffly. "Miss Davenport is exceedingly diligent in obtaining references for all potential staff members."

"Unless you believe the murderer is a student"—Tommy raised his shoulders and held out his hands—"then a murderer on your staff is the only explanation. Of course, a killer amongst your students would also cause Lady Northmoor and myself to worry considerably about your ability to keep Lady Isabelle safe."

"You said yourself these are uncommon times, Lord Northmoor. I can assure you that we have never had such a thing happen before at Docere House. Were you yourself not perfectly safe when you attended school here?"

"I was indeed," Tommy admitted.

"That was Colonel Clark-Biddington on the telephone. He's heard—" Julia Davenport started speaking as soon as she opened the door between the two offices. She stopped when she saw Tommy.

"Good afternoon, Miss Davenport," he said pleasantly. "I trust the colonel is well?"

"He's fine," she replied in a brittle voice.

"Lord Northmoor wants to withdraw the application for Lady Isabelle." Nanny Bunting looked at Tommy as she spoke.

"Oh, for goodness' sake." Julia Davenport shook her head, then pinned Tommy with a frustrated glare. "Are you the reason the colonel is the third parent I have had on the telephone in the last half an hour informing me they wish to withdraw their child?"

"I have made one telephone call while I've been here," he replied. "And that was to my aunt who, I must tell you, was already aware there had been a death at Docere House."

"But how?" She wailed. "How is that even possible?"

Tommy crossed his long legs at the ankles. "I should think that is rather obvious. You have staff who have access to the telephone. The doctor has visited twice, and the police were called. All that is required is for one of those people to tell one other person and every telephone in North Yorkshire would then sound within minutes. One doesn't have to wait for telegrams or the newspaper to find things out these days."

"We shall be ruined." Julia put her hands to her face.

"Perhaps if we catch the killer, disaster can be averted," Tommy suggested.

Julia put out a shaky hand and pointed at Tommy. "If you and your wife hadn't turned up here this morning, this would not be happening."

"I hardly think we are to blame," he said icily.

"If you hadn't gone sniffing around in things that do not concern you, no one would ever have dreamed that Gower's death was anything but a terrible tragedy."

"You are missing the obvious, Miss Davenport," Tommy worked hard to stop his voice from passing over from polite rigidity to outright hostility. "Had someone at Docere House not murdered Captain Gower, there would have been nothing for us to find. You should save your rancour for that person."

"I suppose you are not about to repeat the absurd suggestions your wife made earlier. I tell you, Lord Northmoor, I shall not stand for it."

"Not at all," Tommy said smoothly. "It's quite clear there's a rotten egg at Docere House. Whether that is because someone is an enemy of England, or simply murderous, I will find out. I make no assertions, just promises. That person, or persons, has nowhere to hide."

"Very reassuring, Lord Northmoor." Nanny Bunting got to her feet. "We shall give you a week's grace in regard to Lady Isabelle's admission application. Should we not hear from you within that time, we will destroy the form Lady Northmoor completed."

"I thank you for your consideration." Tommy got to his feet. "But we will not need any further period of contemplation."

He had left the school office and was halfway back to the library before he realised that he hadn't asked Nanny Bunting to look at his hand. He could only hope the detective inspector did not notice it sported no evidence of receiving medical attention.

10

Evelyn could understand Detective Inspector Andrews's insistence that they retire from investigating after the library was deliberately set on fire with them inside, but she was not about to abide by his instructions. They were so close—she could just feel it.

Shortly after Tommy and Detective Inspector Andrews left the library, Clarissa Cambridge arrived. She looked around the room slowly before her gaze fell on Constance.

"How nice it is to see you again, Miss Cambridge," Constance said.

"It's an absolute pleasure to see you again after so long," the headmistress's assistant replied, looking rather unnerved for the first time that day. Perhaps she was just being polite with her greeting because, after all, hadn't she told Tommy she didn't remember either of his sisters?

"Constance is engaged to be married," Grace gushed, looking at her sister with an expression Evelyn had never seen before on the face of the younger girl. There was no doubt Constance and Grace were fond of each other, but the only word Evelyn could use to describe the look on Grace's face was simpering—it was most unlike her.

"Oh, how wonderful," Miss Cambridge answered. "Is the wedding soon?"

"She's marrying the Earl of Chesden," Grace went on. "In Ireland."

Clarissa looked out of the window for a moment and then at Constance, completely ignoring Grace. "I have heard that name."

Of course she had. Everyone knew about the terrible scandal that had befallen the Ryder family a couple of years previously. The previous Earl of Chesden, so the official story went, had momentarily lost control of his senses and committed murder.

The only decent thing he'd done since that awful time in London was declare himself sane repeatedly during his trial. Whilst that saved him from the asylum, it did not save him from the hangman's noose.

Although it was mortifying for both Alexander and David, it allowed them to start rebuilding their family's honour—something they would've found it hard to do with their father languishing in a home for the mentally disturbed.

"As most people have," Evelyn said quietly. "Lord Chesden is part of one of the oldest and most distinguished families in England."

"Of course." Miss Cambridge's tone was deferential, but the look she gave Constance was anything but. "I know from experience how hard it can be to avoid the stain of gossip even though one is completely innocent oneself."

"Are you, perhaps, talking about your poor husband?"

The assistant's brow furrowed as she looked at Evelyn. Then she gave a slight nod as her confusion eased. "Lord Northmoor told you about my husband."

"He did," Evelyn murmured. "How awful for you that people tittle-tattled after his untimely death."

"They talked about every aspect of our relationship," the other woman said bitterly. "Even in his death, they gave us no peace."

"Why?" Grace asked.

Clarissa's gaze flicked to the younger girl. "What do you mean?"

Grace flushed and looked as though she very much regretted her impulsive question. "Why did they talk about you while your husband was alive?

Why did they continue to chatter when he died? I don't understand."

"Some people like nothing more than to tell tales about other people."

"But why?" Grace persisted, impressing Evelyn with her desire to fluster Miss Cambridge despite her own discomfort. "Why did your neighbours talk about you?"

An idea formed in Evelyn's mind, but she kept quiet as she waited for the assistant's answer.

Clarissa's lips formed a hard line. "My husband was somewhat older than me."

"Was that the only reason?" Evelyn pressed. "Or might it have been because he was a foreign national and your neighbours did not trust him?"

"How dare you, Lady Northmoor!" Clarissa Cambridge rounded on Evelyn. "Fred was as English as you and your precious Northmoors and Chesdens."

"Did you meet him at one of the school dances?" Constance spoke up, her voice quiet and measured—a contrast to the anger in Clarissa's and the probing in Evelyn's.

Clarissa let out a long breath. "Yes. That's right."

"I don't remember any older gentlemen attending those dances. They were mostly young local boys of a similar age to our own, with only a few recently enlisted soldiers." Constance tilted her head to one side.

Evelyn couldn't help but admire how both of her sisters-in-law had joined in with her questioning of Clarissa. Although she had planned for an informal discussion that would not give Clarissa any reason to feel uncomfortable, it had quickly turned into an interrogation that clearly had the other woman feeling extremely ill at ease.

"Fred was a senior officer," Clarissa said stiffly. "He chaperoned some of the army youths."

"Did you make your home nearby?" Evelyn asked, firing out another question.

"Scarborough," Clarissa returned. "Have you finished cross-examining me? I was told Constance and Grace wanted to catch up. I was not prepared for, nor expecting, you all to put me through the wringer in the way that you have."

Constance gave a small laugh. "Goodness. I thought we were catching up. Isn't this exactly what one does when they haven't seen an acquaintance for some time? One asks about your life since we last saw you. Isn't it natural that we would ask about your husband, where you lived, and how you have been?"

"That isn't how this feels." Clarissa walked over to the window and stared outside. "It feels like an ambush."

"That's probably my fault," Evelyn said smoothly. "Sometimes I get so focussed on an investigation I forget myself. Please accept my apologies.

Perhaps I should just leave and let you girls chat between yourselves."

"I don't think that Tommy—"

"He wouldn't, Grace." Evelyn smiled at her sister-in-law. "He wouldn't like it at all. So let's just not tell him. I shall be back before he even realises I am gone."

Evelyn walked to the door of the library and was stopped by one of the uniformed police officers. "My lady?"

"I wish to use the convenience," Evelyn said.

"The convenience?"

Evelyn leaned a little closer to the officer and whispered. "The lavatory. I need to visit the lavatory."

"Ah." He pulled at his collar and then looked around with a worried expression on his face. "I should—"

"I do hope you are not about to suggest that you will accompany me?"

"He is not," said a voice from behind Evelyn. "But I shall."

Evelyn turned and smiled. "Thank you, Aunt Em. How wonderful."

The police officer stood back and allowed Evelyn and Aunt Em to leave the library and walk unhindered and unfollowed along the corridor. Tommy's aunt had been so quiet during their conversation with Clarissa Cambridge, she had almost forgotten she was in the room with them.

"The silly man has forgotten the reason he is supposed to be protecting us is because we were attacked in the library. We were not alone when that happened, but in a group." She looked at Evelyn with obvious reproof. "We are not safe, Evelyn. Whatever it is you are about to do is most likely extremely foolhardy."

"I actually think the library was set on fire because we were getting too close to whatever it is that Ralph was trying to tell us," Evelyn said, as they hurried away from the library. "The girls will be fine, as the police will stay there to guard them. We will also be unharmed, as the murderer wants to protect whatever is in the library."

"You hope," Aunt Em muttered. "The murderer may wish to permanently stop us from finding out the rest of Ralph's code."

"Let us hope I am right, and you are wrong!"

"Where are we going?"

"I must talk to Francis Galbraith, but first I need to make an extremely important telephone call. I may need you to distract Nanny Bunting so I can be certain I am not overheard."

"Mr Miller, may I have a word?" Tommy waited outside the man's classroom until his lesson ended before going inside.

The English master looked up from where he was stacking papers on his desk. "Lord Northmoor, I presume? I believe that I had the pleasure of talking to your delightful wife earlier today."

Tommy held out his hand for the elderly school-master to shake. "My wife said she enjoyed your chat immensely. I have a few follow-up questions, if you don't mind?"

Edwin Miller pulled up a couple of chairs and gratefully sank down into one. "Sit down, Lord Northmoor. I will be happy to answer anything you wish to ask me. As I said to Lady Northmoor earlier, although I know Mr Gower reported me to Julia Davenport, I harboured no ill will towards him."

Tommy strode over to close the classroom door before taking the seat next to the teacher. "I am glad to hear it. Perhaps you know that Ralph Gower and I served together?"

"I recall Lady Northmoor referred to him as Captain Gower. That makes more sense to me now knowing you were in the military together. Army?"

"That's right." Tommy shifted uncomfortably on the hard wooden chair.

"You don't like to talk about it." There was sympathy in the other man's eyes. "I understand that. I lost two brothers in the Boer War; another survived. He never once spoke about anything that happened to him overseas. His experiences affected him for the rest of his life."

There was something about Edwin Miller that reminded Tommy of his own father. It wasn't just the sharpness of his gaze, as though he could see right inside to Tommy's innermost thoughts, but he exuded integrity. He very rarely dared to be anything other than completely honest with his father, knowing that he would have spotted an untruth the moment it left his lips.

"I talk about those dark days with our village vicar, and even then infrequently," Tommy admitted. "But no one else. Not even my wife. Especially not my wife."

"You don't wish for her to know the unpleasant things you saw?"

Tommy shook his head. "It's more than that. I never want her to know the man I had to become during those years away from her. She wouldn't like him."

"I believe Lady Northmoor is far more resilient than you give her credit for."

"She is." Tommy gazed at the other man. "Absolutely she is. But that doesn't change my way of thinking. If she knew who I'd been during the war, she would stick by me. Of course she would.

However, she would see me differently, and that is what I could not bear."

"Lady Northmoor told you about my affliction?" the English master changed the subject with a deftness that almost wrong-footed Tommy.

"Your diagnosis of Parkinsons?" Tommy asked. "She did tell me. I am very sorry that your students were so very wrong in their assessment of you."

"I think you must feel a similar way to me," Edwin Miller mused as he looked at Tommy directly. "You don't want your wife to know the secret part of yourself. I didn't want Miss Davenport, or anyone else for that matter, to know that I had Parkinsons. For some reason, admitting what I have, even to myself, makes me feel less of a man."

Grief flooded over Tommy, and he took a moment to gather his thoughts. "War has a way of stripping a man of everything that he believes himself to be and leaving him a mere shadow of his former self."

"That is how I feel," the teacher admitted. "A shadow of who I once was. It's for that reason that I can understand why you would see me as a suspect in the death of your friend. I was quite desperate to keep teaching and not admit to myself, let alone anyone else, that my career and, indeed, my life as I knew it was over."

"You had an excellent motive to want Captain Gower silenced."

"I did. All I can tell you is that I would never do such a thing to a man such as Gower. I told you a moment ago about my brothers. They served this country with distinction. Two of them did not come home. I stayed here, at this school, so I can't pretend to understand what they went through, but I will always be proud of them and their sacrifice."

"Do you feel guilty?" Tommy wondered. "They gave their life for their country, and you have given your life to this school?"

"Not guilty as such, Lord Northmoor," the older man answered. "I don't regret my choice and I'm certain that if my brothers could answer the same question, they would say that they don't regret theirs. However, my respect for men brave enough to do what they did, what you did, and what Gower did, knows no bounds. I am a very patriotic man, and you are all heroes to me."

"How would you feel if you found out there was someone at the school who did not have the best interests of this country at heart?"

Edwin Miller eyed Tommy curiously. "I would, of course, be furious."

"I shall not repeat who said the words, or to whom. Neither will I reveal the person who overheard what was said. However, during our investigations, we have been told that it was stated that national security was being put at risk by this school."

"By whom? In what way?"

"That's just the thing," Tommy said, with as much confusion as the other man. "We don't know. I feel like it is at the very crux of what happened to Captain Gower, possibly even the reason for his murder, but I can't make head nor tail of what it means."

"Were you in Yorkshire in December of 1914?"

"When the Germans attacked Scarborough?"

"Yes."

"I was," Tommy answered. "It was the main reason I enlisted. I couldn't bear the thought that the enemy was attacking where I lived. Scarborough was completely undefended, and civilians died because of the attack."

"There was a lot of talk about enemies, spies, and the like around that time," Edwin Miller said. "I heard nothing specific about the school, but who knows? It's possible someone here gave information to the Germans, given our proximity to Scarborough."

"Who worked at Docere House then that is still here now?" A tremor of excitement ran through Tommy as this new line of enquiry opened up. His enthusiasm, however, was tempered with dread at the possibility of spies living nearby—both during the war and in these days.

"Miss Davenport, her father, and Nanny Bunting were all here. Miss Cambridge was still a student. A couple of old duffers like myself. Most of the masters are new. All the female teachers. The school didn't employ women before the war. Afterwards, it had to."

"I don't suppose you know anything about secret passages in the school?" Tommy asked carefully.

The question was a calculated risk. If Edwin Miller was involved in the murder of Ralph Gower, he was letting the other man know they were uncovering clues. If he wasn't, then as a long-serving member of staff, he could have vital information to share with them.

Edwin Miller gave a dry laugh. "There's always talk with buildings as old as this one. It is said that there's a secret passage in the library. I don't know how true that is. I'm afraid I don't even recall where, or from whom, I heard that."

"Thank you, Mr Miller." Tommy didn't confirm that the rumour tallied with the information they had from the clues Ralph had left.

"Don't you want to ask me questions about where I was when Gower died? That sort of thing?"

"I don't think that I need to," Tommy said.

"Because a man such as myself, with uncontrollable tremors, couldn't have killed him?"

"No," Tommy replied. "It has nothing to do with your illness but everything to do with who you are as a person."

“You should be careful who you trust, my lord,” the teacher warned. “Everything I have just told you could be a lie to hide my criminal proclivity.”

“You’re right,” Tommy said grimly. “It could be, but I don’t believe that you are a liar or an immoral and dishonourable man.”

Edwin Miller shook his head sadly. “Please do not dismiss anyone as a suspect simply because you like them. Murderers are generally rather good at hiding in plain sight or perhaps even pretending they are an innocent and somewhat doddery old fellow such as myself.”

Tommy smiled dourly. “Don’t worry, Mr Miller. This isn’t my first experience of facing suspects I like very much.”

“You were forced to apprehend someone you liked?”

“In a manner of speaking,” Tommy replied, recalling the time an old family friend had committed a series of murders to cover up blackmail. He remembered how angry Evelyn had been with him, as she believed Tommy had allowed the perpetrator to take the easy way out. She much preferred to see justice was meted out by the police and the court process. “If I may ask you one more question?”

“Please do.”

“Where have you been for the last hour?”

“It was my pleasure”—the man’s face twisted

into a wry grimace at the last word—"to spend that time teaching the upper sixth the joys of *Hamlet*."

"Gilbert Wellesley is in the upper sixth?"

"That is correct." He nodded. "Good luck, Lord Northmoor."

Tommy left the classroom eager to get back to the library. While he believed his sisters had no intention of leaving the room in which they were meeting Clarissa Cambridge, he was under no such illusions about Evelyn. Goodness only knew what she had been getting up to.

With no pretence at calmness, he jogged back to the main school, his thoughts full of secret passages, spies, and the treachery of men.

Evelyn paused outside Nanny Bunting's office. "Are you clear about what I need you to do?"

"My dear." Aunt Em gave Evelyn one of her most superior looks. "I've been manipulating people to suit my own needs since before you were even born."

Evelyn did not hide her smile of amusement. Aunt Em could always be relied upon to lighten the mood when investigations were getting too complex. Evelyn knocked on the door to the secretary's office and followed the nanny's direction to enter.

"Lady Northmoor." Nanny Bunting pursed her lips as though she were sucking a particularly tart lemon. "What can I do for you?"

"I wonder if I might be permitted to use the telephone?" Evelyn asked. "I'm afraid the police are no longer happy for us to remain here at Docere House, given the very real threat to our lives. Detective Inspector Andrews has insisted that we go home. I need to ask our chauffeur to collect us immediately."

"Go ahead." The secretary indicated the instrument on the edge of her desk, then looked at Aunt Em with interest.

"Perhaps I could have a moment of your time?" Aunt Em asked, then added in a stage whisper, "Out in the corridor—I have something to discuss with you that may be of benefit to the school."

Evelyn pretended she had not heard Aunt Em as she walked over to the telephone. She waited until she was sure Nanny Bunting had left the room with Aunt Em to place her call to Hessleham Hall.

"Malton?"

"Lady Northmoor," the butler replied is his usual calm and efficient way. "How can I help you?"

"Has Albert set off to collect us yet?"

"I believe he has just returned to Hessleham Hall, my lady."

"Perfect," Evelyn said. "Now I need you to listen

very carefully to what I am about to say. It is utterly imperative that you repeat what I say to Albert and that he understands exactly what I am asking him to do."

"Of course, my lady."

"There is a young lady here at Docere House by the name of Clarissa Cambridge. She married a fellow named Fred. I'm afraid I know no more about his name, but I do know that she was significantly younger than him. The lady in question is a similar age to Miss Constance. I need Albert to ask at the churches in Scarborough to find out more about this marriage. Fred was an army officer, so hopefully that will help jog someone's memory. They would have married during the war."

"Does this have something to do with poor Captain Gower's death?"

"It does," Evelyn said in a serious tone. "When Albert returns to Docere House, he must see me first whether or not he has found out any information about Miss Cambridge and her husband. He must bring with him a piece of paper in an envelope. After he has spoken to me, he will give the envelope to Lord Northmoor and tell his lordship that it is an urgent telegram which was received at Hessleham Hall and that he, Albert, believes contains extremely important information pertinent to our investigation."

"I understand, Lady Northmoor." Malton's confusion was apparent in his short sentence.

"I'm sure this must seem rather ridiculous to you," she said.

"Not at all, my lady."

"You are too kind," Evelyn told him. "I know it's rather a jumble, but it's very important that we get this right."

"You can rely on us," he said firmly. "I hope you know that, my lady."

"I certainly do." Evelyn cast a look towards the closed office door. "Thank you, Malton. Now do please excuse me, I must rescue the school secretary from Lady Emily."

Evelyn walked back into the corridor, where she found Aunt Em in deep conversation with Nanny Bunting. The latter turned towards Evelyn with a distinctly sly smile on her face.

"I enjoyed our chat immensely, Lady Emily," the secretary gushed.

Aunt Em reached out and patted the other woman on the arm. "You just leave things with me. I will be in touch."

The outer door flew open, and Gilbert Wellesley rushed in and skidded to a stop in front of Evelyn. "Lady Northmoor! I must speak to you. I've been speaking to my pals—"

"Yes, yes!" Evelyn said loudly as she spoke over

the top of the sixth former's excitement. "Let's take a walk in the grounds."

"But I simply must tell you—"

Evelyn gripped the boy's elbow and propelled him towards the door. "And so you shall. Outside."

Gilbert finally seemed to understand that Evelyn didn't want him to say anything while they were still in the school building. He giggled and placed a finger against his lips. "Understood."

"Did everything go according to plan?" Evelyn asked Aunt Em.

"Of course," Em replied indignantly, as though there could never have been any doubt. "Nanny Bunting believes I will use my influence on you and Tommy, so that you reinstate Isabelle's name on the school's waiting list."

Evelyn shook her head. "I don't know if that is a sign of how clever you are or how gullible Nanny Bunting is."

"Come now, dear." Em linked an arm through Evelyn's as they followed Gilbert Wellesley out onto the lawn in front of the school. "I think we both know the answer to that conundrum."

"May I now speak?" Gilbert practically bounced on his feet in front of the two women.

She looked back towards the school and saw Tommy staring moodily out of the library window in their direction. Evelyn raised a hand and gave him a small wave. She doubted that would improve his disposition. He would be furious she hadn't stayed in the library. If Detective Inspector Andrews saw her and realised she was still actively sleuthing, he would be positively apoplectic. She couldn't really blame either man for their anger with her.

"You may."

"Simmons, he's one of my best—"

Evelyn shook her head. "No background required, Wellesley. Just the facts. We have no time to lose."

The boy let out a long breath. "Simmons overheard Mr Gower talking to himself. To be honest, we both thought he was rather batty lately. There were definitely a few bats loose in his belfry this term."

"Wellesley!"

He licked his lips and looked nervously at Evelyn. "Sorry, Lady Northmoor. I keep forgetting he was a friend of yours. But if you had seen him walking around muttering away to absolutely no one, you would better understand what I'm talking about."

"He had a lot on his mind."

"He certainly did! Gosh, if I thought the same as him, I would've been positively nutty too. He was behaving as though he was a character in one of those rather spiffing detective novels."

"Boy!" Aunt Em's voice cracked through the still

air like a whip. "Please stop prevaricating and tell us what you know. Immediately."

"Mr Gower was trying to decide what to do. He said there was a spy at the school, and it was up to him to make sure national security was not compromised. There was something Simmons couldn't quite hear. Then he mumbled that he accepted the responsibility of smoking out the enemy to England from the school. Simmons said it was rather as though Mr Gower was speaking to someone that only he could see."

Aunt Em looked at Evelyn with both regret and sadness. "It sounds like the boy might be right. Perhaps Captain Gower had simply taken leave of his senses and all this business about spies is the ramblings of a deeply disturbed mind."

"Do you think it's all nonsense?" Evelyn asked. "The codes, the idea of a spy at the school, that Captain Gower thought it was his duty to uncover the spy's identity?"

"Is it a secret code? Do you have clues?" The youth asked with great interest. "Perhaps Simmons and I can solve it for you? We're both rather good at solving maths problems."

Evelyn wished she had not spoken in front of the boy. The last thing they needed was the upper sixth rushing around the school trying to look for clues.

She held up a hand. "The police are investigating. There's already talk about several parents removing their children from school for their own safety, so if you want to remain here, you should refrain from involving yourself in the death of Captain Gower."

He stuck out his bottom lip and looked at Evelyn in obvious confusion. "But isn't that what you asked me to do?"

"Absolutely not," she said. "I simply asked you if you knew anything about his behaviour recently. Surely you want to keep your head down, and work hard, so your father can be told what a splendid chap you are?"

"Indeed I do," he said stoutly. "It wouldn't do for Father to get wind of *anything* that's happened here recently."

Evelyn almost felt sorry for the boy as he looked at her with such hope in his expression. "Don't worry, Wellesley. I have it on good authority that your father will not find out about that spot of bother you had with your science examination. However, if you were to put a foot wrong, and not heed my warning, I cannot guarantee that he would not hear about the whole sorry incident."

His face broke out into a wide grin, and he looked for a moment like he wanted to vigorously shake Evelyn's hand. Fortunately, he remembered himself and schooled his face into more respectful lines. "May I be excused?"

"Of course." Evelyn returned his smile. "But remember what I said: no interfering and no more cheating."

"Thank you, Lady Northmoor," he called over his shoulder as he jogged away from her. "You're a jolly good sort."

11

"Where have you been?" Tommy asked, taking great pains to keep his tone calm and non-accusatory.

"I'm so sorry if you were worried, darling," Evelyn replied as she entered the library with Aunt Em. "I realised we hadn't telephoned home to ask for Albert to bring the motor car back."

"I believe the police were taking care of that task."

Evelyn lifted a shoulder. "I thought they might forget."

Tommy did not think that was very likely, but he allowed Evelyn's suggestion to go unchecked. "I assume you had an ulterior motive for making the call?"

"Of course," she said smoothly. "I realised that Em's contact who gets information from Somerset

House might find it difficult to get the information we need because we do not know the full name of Clarissa Cambridge's husband."

"Do you think she has something to do with this?" Constance asked.

"I think it is possible. Fred is an unknown, so it's important we find out as much as we can about him," Evelyn answered, then turned to her husband. "There is so much we must share with you, Tommy."

"Did you solve the clue on the paper I found underneath the desk?"

"We did. The three words are, spy, secret, and passage."

His heart beat a painful rhythm against his rib cage. Simply hearing the word 'spy' reminded him of the terrible times during the war when one could never be absolutely certain who to trust and who was working for both sides.

More pertinently, it reminded him of the reason he had chosen to fight for his country—the Germans had planned the naval attack on Scarborough with precision. It had long been feared that information about the location of the British fleet, and the relative lack of defences around Scarborough, had led to the assault on the coastal town.

"So Ralph's clues tell us that someone poisoned him with berries and, most likely, it was because they were a spy and he somehow uncovered that information?"

"Is it at all possible that he *knew* there was a spy here?" Evelyn asked.

"Before he took up the position of science master, do you mean?"

"Yes." She nodded. "Given his background, could Ralph's work here have been a cover, and he was actually on an assignment to find a spy?"

It didn't take long for Tommy to give an answer —he had come to the same conclusion himself only moments earlier. "That would make sense. However, was it the government or Ralph's decision to poison the spy, rather than bring him in to face justice?"

"You can't think that was his intention?" Grace gasped. "Surely there was another reason."

He understood his sister's reluctance to believe what was staring them in the face. Grace hadn't known Ralph Gower, but even so, she found it difficult to believe he could have made taxine for nefarious reasons. Tommy knew far worse things had happened during the war.

"I wish that wasn't a possibility," he answered eventually. "I can see no logical reason Captain Gower would make taxine unless he intended to use it to kill someone."

"I think we need to go over again what we know," Evelyn suggested. He watched as she repressed a shudder and drew her shoulders up. "Someone deliberately threw a lit oil lamp onto the rug and then locked us in this very room. That must be because the perpetrator believes we are getting too near their identity."

"Bertie was with me," Tommy said. "But, of course, that doesn't mean he isn't working with someone else and that person, or persons, started the fire."

"Are we to assume the spy and the person who killed Ralph may not be the same person?" Aunt Em asked astutely.

"If Ralph was correct," Tommy said, "and I have no reason to doubt his belief that there was a spy here, then Ralph's murder could well be part of a bigger conspiracy or cover-up. That certainly points to more than one person."

"Let's go through our suspects," Evelyn suggested. "Who could have thrown the oil lamp? You've already suggested it probably wasn't Bertie Adams acting alone, Tommy."

"What did you learn from Gilbert Wellesley?" he asked. "I assume that is the young man I saw you talking to on the lawn?"

"When I spoke to Gilbert, he had just come from a lesson. Obviously, I haven't been able to verify that information with anyone, but I would imagine it would be easy enough for the police to confirm that."

"Edwin Miller had an English lesson after lunch with the upper sixth. I met with him in his classroom. He could not have got over here and set the fire if he was teaching. Presumably as Gilbert is in the upper sixth, and would have been in that lesson, neither could he."

"We need to speak to the police again," Constance said firmly. "They can check the validity of alibis while we work on locating the secret passage."

Once again, Tommy was struck with the reality that his sisters were no longer innocent schoolgirls. They were grown women who not only knew their own minds, but their minds were mature and logical.

"That's a very sensible idea, my dear." Aunt Em nodded her agreement.

The pieces of paper containing the codes they had found so far were on the table. Grace tapped the paper with her fingertips. "If those alibis hold, that leaves us with Miss Davenport, Nanny Bunting, and Clarissa Cambridge."

"Nanny Bunting is very loyal to the Davenport family," Evelyn said. "She told me she has been with the family since Julia was a baby."

"Perhaps one should bear in mind the previous incident we are aware of involving the Davenport family." Aunt Em raised an eyebrow at Tommy. "Herbert Davenport previously lost this school in a reckless bet with your Uncle Charles. My recollection of those times is that he was quite the inveterate gambler."

"One can only imagine who else he may have lost a game of cards with," Evelyn murmured.

"My thoughts exactly," Tommy said grimly.

"Let's do our best to find the secret passage." Evelyn got to her feet and walked over to the burned wooden floor where the rug had lain before it was set on fire.

"I shall help you in a moment," Tommy said as he walked over to the door. "I will ask the police officer outside if he can let Detective Inspector Andrews know that we have learned new information. It would be extremely helpful if they use their resources to confirm that none of our male suspects could have set the fire."

Evelyn leaned down to knock on the scorched wood, but nothing happened. She had wondered if the reason the oil lamp had been thrown was because they were, quite literally, too close, but it appeared it was simply because the rug was flammable.

The girls were systematically pulling books forward and running their fingers along the wooden shelves at the back of the volumes. Evelyn moved across the floor, tapping at the wood with her shoes. Aunt Em stood in the middle of the room looking around her.

"It must be easier than that," she said with a frown. "Surely if Captain Gower found the secret passage, he either did so accidentally or actually saw someone go into it?"

"Do you think we're being too systematic?" Tommy asked as he walked back into the room.

"I think we're searching for a secret passage that we know is hidden," she replied. "How would Gower have known there was a secret passage, or that it was relevant?"

"If he watched someone vanish into it, he can have only done that through either the window or the open door," Evelyn said. "If a person was intending to go into the secret passage, they would close the door, so what they were doing remained a secret."

"The groom did mention to us that Ralph liked to walk around the grounds," Tommy remembered.

Evelyn looked out of the window. "We've both walked on the lawn outside. Aunt Em is right. If the mechanism opened by moving a book, you wouldn't see which book it was from outside. In fact, you'd struggle to pinpoint accurately which shelf the person was touching."

Aunt Em looked outside and then walked up to the mantelpiece. Grasping one of the lion's head ornaments that sat at each edge, she pulled it towards her. A grating sound filled the room, and one large block of bookcases slowly moved to the left, revealing a concealed doorway.

"Aunt Em!" Grace exclaimed. "How did you know?"

"I had an old friend who had a similar system in the library in his house. We had hours of fun hiding from his nanny." She smiled at the memory. "She later told us that she had searched the grounds for us for hours and was about to tell his mother that we were both missing when we reappeared."

"Didn't you know she was looking for you?"

"We presumed she would be," Aunt Em replied. "Eventually we came out because we were jolly hungry."

"I can't imagine you as a naughty little girl," Constance said, looking at her great aunt in awe.

"Can't you, dear?" Em gave what could only be described as a mischievous smile. "How very disappointing."

Still smiling at the exchange, Evelyn hurried over to the door.

"Shouldn't we wait for the police?"

Evelyn didn't need to turn around to know it was Constance who had spoken. Grace seemed rather caught up in the excitement of spies, and catching a killer, whereas Constance seemed much more worried about doing something for which she could get into trouble.

That was understandable given her upcoming nuptials and the fact her fiancé's family had only recently been embroiled in a terrible scandal. The last thing Constance would want was for there to be further disgrace heaped on the Ryder family name.

"I informed the police officer we needed to speak to Detective Inspector Andrews," Tommy said. "I'm sure he will be along very soon."

Evelyn turned to look at Tommy, and as he nodded in her direction, she twisted the brass doorknob and pushed open the door.

Tentatively, almost as though someone were going to jump out and grab her, she stepped inside. It was dank and musty, the air stale. It was also rather too dark to see anything other than brick walls and a stone floor.

"Evelyn?" Tommy's voice came from over her right shoulder.

"I can't see anything." She backed up and stepped back into the library. "There's no light in there."

"Perhaps that's why there are still old oil lamps at Docere House," he suggested. "Whoever makes it a habit to come in here knows that they need one to see whatever it is they keep in here."

"What do you think is in there?" Grace wondered.

"Perhaps documents, maps, letters. Something of that sort." Tommy shrugged. "If, of course, this is where the spy hides their things."

The library door opened and Detective Inspector Andrews came into the room. "What do we have here, then?"

"A secret passage," Evelyn replied, then grimaced. It was plainly obvious what it was.

"What's inside?"

She shrugged. "It's too dark to see."

The detective opened the door and stuck his head out. She could hear him murmuring to someone outside, then the sound of running feet, before he closed the door again and turned back to her. "Perhaps you had better tell me everything you have learned since lunch. I distinctly remember telling you not to investigate."

Evelyn gave him her brightest smile. "We're here in the library, where you told us to stay."

"I see that," he retorted. "But staying in one room is not the same as ceasing your investigations, is it?"

"I'm sure I don't know what you mean."

Whatever the detective was about to say next was cut off by the door opening once more and Detective Sergeant Montgomery coming in with a lit oil lamp.

"Where did you get that from?" Tommy asked urgently.

"The secretary." The detective passed the lamp to his superior. "And let me tell you, she was none too happy about it."

"More likely than not, she is involved in this," Tommy told Detective Inspector Andrews as Evelyn stood back to allow the detective access to the secret room.

"The nanny?" he asked, incredulity coating each syllable. "Why would she want to kill a school-teacher?"

"We shall explain everything," Tommy assured him. "After you have seen what is inside."

Evelyn exchanged a look with Tommy as the detective entered the hidden room with the lamp held out in front of him. Moments later, he exited, a look of consternation on his face.

"What is it?" she asked desperately. "What's in there?"

"I don't know what you were expecting to find," he said tersely. "But whatever it is, it isn't in there. The room is empty."

12

"There must be something," Tommy insisted.

"I tell you," the detective insisted. "There's nothing."

Tommy moved forward as though to pass the detective and see for himself, but the policeman put out a hand. "You cannot go in there. There's nothing in there now, but there was until very recently."

"How can you tell?"

"There are marks in the dust that show something was once there."

"There should be another clue in there," Tommy said desperately.

"If there was, it's not there now."

Fury boiled through Tommy. They were too late! Whoever it was had got there before them and covered their tracks. Deflated, he pulled out one chair that sat around the large table near the mantelpiece.

Evelyn moved to his side and rested a hand on his shoulder. “This is not over.”

He was heartened by his wife’s words, but he could see no way forward. How could they find out what exactly Ralph was telling them if the last clue was missing? Not to mention whatever had been in the hidden room.

Grace pulled a sheet of paper from the pile in the middle of the desk towards her and picked up a discarded pen. After a few tentative strokes on the top sheet to ensure it worked, she looked at Tommy. “Let’s list everything we know about Captain Gower.”

Although he was proud of his sister’s tenacity, he couldn’t see how it would help. Never had he felt more defeated than he did at that moment.

Constance sat on the chair next to her sister. “He was a code breaker during the war.”

Aunt Em sat opposite. “He was a patriotic and honourable man.”

“Ralph was a planner,” Evelyn said. “He left a trail for us to follow, even though he must have been frightened for his life. Numerous people told us that his behaviour was irrational, out of the norm for him, and that he acted as though he was being followed.”

“All perfectly understandable if the poor fellow

thought someone was trying to silence him," Tommy said morosely.

Grace's pen scratched along the paper as she made notes. "What else?"

"He liked to walk around the grounds," he said, encouraged by his family's enthusiasm for the task. "Ralph did not trust Clarissa Cambridge and warned Francis Galbraith that she was dangerous."

"He liked to paint," Evelyn said. "He painted the picture in his living room."

"I didn't know that." Detective Inspector Andrews leaned over Grace's shoulder and read what she'd written. "What is the painting of?"

"It's a sort of landscape," Evelyn answered. Tommy was glad that she had taken more notice of it than he had—he was ashamed that he had barely given the artwork a second glance. "It's of the school and buildings with a couple of horses in the distance. I rather liked it."

"Bertie Adams told us that Julia Davenport was angry or frustrated with Ralph," Tommy said.

"The maid said she overheard something about national security," Aunt Em added. "That must certainly be relevant."

"Gilbert Wellesley told me that Bertie Adams often brought Captain Gower coffee." Evelyn squeezed Tommy's shoulder. Her strength sustained him and filled him with renewed confidence that they would prevail.

"Bertie admitted he was trying to make taxine and that he was jealous of Ralph," Tommy said. "Though, in his defence, he seemed genuinely upset about his death and particularly about the fire. In fact, he was instrumental in organising the sand buckets to extinguish it."

"Do we all agree that there was something in that secret room that would point to the killer of Captain Gower?" Detective Inspector Andrews asked, seeming to forget that he was not in his police station surrounded by his colleagues.

"Or perhaps the identity of the killer was clear from whatever was in there," Tommy mused.

"I read a jolly exciting book last month." Grace put down her pen and looked at Tommy, her cheeks bright with excitement. "It was about a chap who worked in Room 40. He was always reminding his colleagues that spies, British spies you know, were taught to trust no one, but that they should always leave a last letter for their loved ones."

"I think that's what he was doing." Tommy smiled kindly at his sister, knowing that she meant well even though she was recounting a tale of fiction. "When he was in bed, immediately prior to his death, he wrote to me."

"What if that wasn't it?" she asked breathlessly. "What if that letter was exactly what it seemed to be —a letter to you because he knew he was dying and he was afraid no one would know his death was murder, but he wanted to leave something behind that he hoped you would understand."

"Let us presume Grace is right." Evelyn increased the pressure on his shoulder. "Just for a moment. We haven't found such a missive. Where might he have left it?"

The room was silent as everyone went over the facts Grace had outlined on the paper in front of her.

"You said he painted, Ev. What is the painting like that you saw in his rooms?" Constance asked.

"I told you, it's of—"

"No, I don't mean what's in it." Constance waved a hand. "I mean, is it any good?"

"It's very sweet," Evelyn said doubtfully.

"Doesn't it strike you as rather self-important for Captain Gower to have displayed a painting done by himself in his accommodation? From what you've told us, it doesn't appear he's that sort of fellow."

"He's not," Tommy said, warming to his sister's idea.

"He was extremely poorly, possibly even knew he was dying," Constance said. "Doesn't it stand to reason that if he was to leave a last letter, as Grace suggested, that it would be close by?"

"This is all rather far-fetched conjecture," Detective Inspector Andrews said doubtfully. "It sounds much more suited to a work of fiction than real life."

"And yet, what do any of us know about spying,

or how those in the intelligence service lived their lives?" Tommy asked. "He would have wanted to do anything in his power to ensure that whoever the spy was, they got caught. I think Grace and Constance's idea is worth exploring further."

The detective held out his hands in supplication. "Lead on, Lord Northmoor. I don't think there's any merit in this idea, but it won't hurt to look at the picture or his room one more time."

"You should stay here," Detective Inspector Andrews said to his subordinate. "I need you to ensure no one goes near the secret passage. It may be a little late, but who knows what the murderer could try next."

"I shall keep you company." Aunt Em eyed the two detectives imperiously, lest they should dare to argue with her. "I would only slow you down."

"I would be delighted." The junior detective said in a voice that suggested he thought the very opposite.

As they all walked over to Elm House, Evelyn couldn't help but wonder what had been removed from the secret passageway—and by whom. The list of suspects had been narrowed significantly from the start of their investigations, but there was still so much they did not know. Certainly, whatever was missing from the hiding place was of great significance.

She hoped that there was something in the painting idea. She hated when Tommy's mood was affected by things that reminded him of a time he would much rather forget.

Although, she didn't necessarily agree that Tommy pretending those things didn't happen was a good thing. In her opinion, a problem shared was a problem halved, but she had long since given up trying to persuade Tommy of her belief. He needed to deal with his emotions in a way that worked for him.

When they arrived at the building, Detective Inspector Andrews led the way up the stairs. Outside the science master's room, he produced a key and unlocked the door.

"Does anyone else have a key to this room?" Evelyn asked.

"I was assured not," he replied.

"By whom?"

"Miss Davenport," the detective answered. "And quite adamantly by Nanny Bunting."

Evelyn made no comment but doubted very much whether the detective had been told the truth. She only hoped Captain Gower's room had not been successfully ransacked in the same way as the secret passage had.

The small living space was crowded by the time

they had all filed in. Grace immediately walked up to the painting and peered closely at it. “I see what you mean, Ev. It is rather sweet.”

“The groom told us Captain Gower spent some time walking the grounds and particularly enjoyed being around the horses—he said it reminded him of his time in the army,” Tommy recalled. “It’s a very peaceful painting, I think.”

Evelyn gripped his hand, offering him the only comfort she could. “Yes, I agree. Now, should we take it down from the wall and see if there’s anything at the back?”

The detective cleared his throat, put on a pair of gloves, and stepped around Grace. “Step back, miss.”

He lifted the picture down to a collective gasp. Printed on the wall behind the picture was another set of codes.

The codes on the wall are:

L6:16,14 (Traitor)
N13:16,12 (Spy)
1K21:23,3 (Jezebel)

“The Bible!” Tommy exclaimed. “Where is

Captain Gower's Bible?"

"The one he was reading when he...um..." the detective paused delicately. "When he expired?"

"Yes, that one," Tommy said urgently. "Where is it?"

The detective lifted a shoulder, not seeming to grasp the importance of locating the book. "I suspect it's still in his bedroom."

In two long strides, Tommy was at the bedroom door and twisting the brass knob to open it. "It's here. Can I bring it through?"

"I see no reason why not," the detective replied, casting an uncertain look at Evelyn. "We don't think the murderer has touched the Bible. Do we?"

Evelyn wanted to laugh at the detective's use of the word 'we', but the desperation in Tommy's voice took away any absurdity and left only his desire to solve the murder of his comrade.

Tommy brought the Bible back through to the living area and, using the same process as previously, they flipped rapidly through the books of the Bible, quickly realising the second code was one they had solved previously: spy. The first was traitor, the last, Jezebel.

"What's Jezebel?" Detective Inspector Andrews asked.

"She was an immoral woman," Grace answered quickly. "A truly wicked *woman*."

"He's telling us the killer is a woman?" the detective asked doubtfully.

"He seems to be." Tommy stared at the words Ralph had written on the wall. "We have three possibilities."

"Julia Davenport, Nanny Bunting, and Clarissa Cambridge." Evelyn counted the women on her fingers.

"Everyone said how sweet Miss Cambridge is, and I must say that I agree." The detective looked at Evelyn. "She's a thoroughly pleasant young woman and I can't see how she can possibly be involved."

Tommy stalked to the door and threw it open. His footsteps sounded loudly in the corridor outside. Evelyn glanced hopelessly at the open door. Her husband clearly needed a few moments by himself. She fought every instinct she had to go after him and offer whatever consolation he would allow.

"There's nothing on the back of the painting," Grace said, disappointment clear in her words. "Can we have a look around to see if we can see anything that might help?"

Detective Inspector Andrews gave Grace the same indulgent look he'd given her earlier. Clearly, he thought women were capable of little intelligence, whether it was in solving crimes or being the perpetrator of them.

Constance and Grace began looking around the room while Evelyn stared at the words on the wall, willing the pieces of the puzzle to join together and reveal to her who had killed Ralph Gower.

"Detective?" Constance called from the bedroom. "What do we know about this letter?"

"The one on the bedside table? It has no evidentiary value."

Constance walked into the living room, holding it out to Detective Inspector Andrews. "May we read it?"

"I don't see why not." He shrugged. "It's just a letter from a mother to her son."

"Tommy!" Evelyn called.

He hurried back into the room. "What is it?"

"Constance has found a letter to Ralph from his mother."

"Is that the one we saw earlier? On his nightstand?"

"It is." Evelyn gestured towards her sister-in-law. "Detective Inspector Andrews said Constance can read it."

Constance smiled tentatively at her brother and drew the letter from its envelope. "*Ralph, I read in my Bible this morning a passage that I thought might help you. It is Matthew 6:33-34. It reads, 'But seek ye first the kingdom of God, and his righteousness; and all these things shall be added unto you. Take therefore no thought for the morrow: for the morrow shall take thought for the things of itself. Sufficient unto the day is the evil thereof.' Please follow Him and seek out His house whenever you are troubled. Mother.* Someone has underlined the words 'seek ye first the kingdom of God'."

Tommy held out his hand. "Can I see that?"

Constance handed the single sheet of paper to Tommy, who gave a firm nod and then passed it to Evelyn.

"More Bible stuff." The detective shook his head. "I don't understand a word of that book. It's everywhere in this case, which makes it even more perplexing for a fellow like me."

"It's quite simple," Grace told him. "Very crudely, the verse means you should put religion at the forefront of your life and not worry about tomorrow, as your future is not in your hands, but in God's."

"I can't trust my future to a being I cannot see."

"You must have more faith, Detective Inspector," Grace said. "That's what is helping us solve this case."

Evelyn wanted to point out that it was also their superior detective skills, but that would be boastful, rude, and unhelpful. Especially because, at that moment, they were as confused as the detective.

She looked down at the short note in her hands and then back at her husband, finally seeing what he must have noticed as soon as he looked at the written words.

Her hands shook as she passed the letter back.

"Is that the same handwriting as that on Captain Gower's army service record card?"

Detective Inspector Andrews held up a hand. "Now wait a minute. I thought you said the words added to the record were written by Captain Gower?"

"Indeed," Tommy said.

"Are you suggesting that Gower wrote that note to himself?" He nodded towards the sheet of paper in Tommy's hands.

"Yes." Tommy nodded. "It would also explain why there's no affection in either the greeting or the closing. One would expect something along the lines of 'My dearest Ralph' and 'Your loving Mother' or suchlike."

"Perhaps they weren't very close." The detective held out his hand for the note and then perused its contents for himself. "What's the clue here, then? I just don't see it."

"I think we need to visit the chapel," Evelyn suggested. "Perhaps there is something to find there."

She could only admire the amount, and variation, of clues that Ralph had left for them. Evelyn tried not to think about the desperation the poor man must have felt as he thought of inventive ways to leave a trail behind him, even as he knew his life was in mortal danger.

Detective Inspector Andrews kept up a monologue about his failings as a 'good Christian man' all the way from Elm House to the small chapel behind the stables.

Tommy refrained from telling the detective that being a Christian wasn't something one could be because they thought they should—it was a deep and irrevocable belief that could only be sustained by an unfailing faith.

"Where should we look?" Grace asked as they entered the old building.

"It will not be anywhere out in the open, otherwise the vicar, or whoever gives the services here, would have found it before now." Tommy ran a hand through his hair. "Perhaps underneath something like the code in the library?"

Constance looked at the stone floor doubtfully before grabbing a kneeler and planted it resolutely in front of the pew facing the pulpit. Grace copied her sister's actions and took the next row, and soon enough, they were all peering underneath the wooden seating.

Finally, Evelyn called out from the very last row. "Here, there's a letter attached to the underside."

Detective Inspector Andrews got to his feet and hurried over. He put on gloves before removing the letter and drawing out another sheet of paper. "It looks like a similar hand to the letter on the nightstand."

"What does it say?" Tommy demanded.

The detective barely paused before deciding to read the letter out loud. "*If you are reading this letter, then I am almost certainly dead. I can only hope that my last words are being read by someone who loves England as fervently as I. My love for my country is why I accepted this mission without pause: locate the spy and eliminate the enemy by any means possible. I did not know then how the reality of killing with my own hands would affect me. Too many times, I hesitated. My mind plays cruel tricks on me, and it often seems to me that everyone is involved and wants me dead. I successfully completed half of my mission. I uncovered the spy and found the evidence in the secret passage in the library. I failed to commit the final, and necessary, act. My reluctance to remove the threat has almost certainly led to my fate. I leave you with the words of Wilfred Owen and pray that you, reader, will have the courage that I did not possess.*

'My friend, you would not tell with such high zest. To children ardent for some desperate glory, The old Lie: Dulce et decorum est Pro patria mori.'"

"It is sweet and beautiful to die for your country." Grace's voice cracked as she translated the Latin sentence at the end of the quote. "Oh, that poor, poor man."

"Do you know?" Detective Inspector Andrews

looked at Tommy and Evelyn. “Do you know who killed him?”

“I know one thing,” Tommy said with certainty. “The person who killed Captain Gower could not possibly have been the same person who was the spy.”

He frowned. “How so?”

“He knew the identity of the spy.” Tommy’s voice vibrated with emotion. “He would not have permitted that person to get close enough to poison him.”

“There’s two killers?”

“One spy, one killer, and one person complicit in everything,” Evelyn stated with conviction.

13

Detective Inspector Andrews had gathered everyone in the library. Purposefully, he had left the door to the secret passage open to gauge people's reaction as they walked in.

Edwin Miller was the only one who commented, though Evelyn noticed his were not the only pair of eyes who strayed to that part of the room. "Goodness me, so it wasn't simply a myth. There actually is a secret passage at the school! Am I allowed to ask what was inside?"

"Nothing," the senior detective answered in a voice that brooked no argument. "There's nothing in the secret passage."

Slowly, suspects, witnesses, and family members took a seat around the table. Evelyn had taken the opportunity to speak to their chauffeur,

Albert, before the senior detective had called the meeting. The information he shared had strengthened what she already knew. At last, the killer of Captain Ralph Gower was about to be uncovered.

The two detectives stood in front of the fireplace with Evelyn and Tommy off to the side in front of the window. A loud knock sounded on the door and Detective Sergeant Montgomery walked over to answer the summons.

"I have a telegram for Lord Northmoor," Albert said in a loud, clear voice, just as he had been instructed. "It is urgent news in relation to the case he has been working on."

Tommy stepped forward to take the envelope from Albert's hand. "Hopefully this will give us the answers to some questions that we have been asking ourselves."

Although Evelyn had been expecting the move, had even hoped for it, she was startled as Clarissa Cambridge rushed from her chair and grabbed the envelope from Tommy's hand. Tearing the envelope open, she then stared at Tommy and Evelyn with her mouth slightly agape.

"Miss Cambridge?" Tommy enquired coolly.

"I thought...that is..." she stammered, then bowed her head. "Please forgive me, my lord. I am afraid that this rather bizarre gathering has me quite flummoxed."

"Perhaps you were expecting the envelope to contain details of your marriage?" Evelyn asked.

The other woman raised her head to stare at Evelyn, the hate in her blue eyes making them almost navy. "I don't know what you mean."

"I think you do, Mrs Marchant."

Clarissa gasped, then stumbled. She reached out for the corner of the table to steady herself. "I...I don't—"

"You were married to Commander Frederick Marchant in the summer of 1914."

"Commander?" Detective Inspector Andrews looked at Tommy as though it hadn't been Evelyn who'd spoken. "Her husband was a Navy Commander? I thought he was in the army?"

"So?" Clarissa raised a shoulder in defiance and regathered some of her usual poise. "What does that matter? I told you my husband was named Fred and that he died."

"Your husband," Evelyn said, unable to keep the vitriol from her voice, "killed himself when he realised you had passed on information on the whereabouts of the British Navy. The attack on Scarborough on the sixteenth of December, 1914, happened only because the Germans knew that several towns along the northeast coast were not adequately defended."

"That is not true!" Clarissa stated as she flopped

back into her chair. "I told you that Fred was devastated by what he had seen during the war and could not cope with the memories."

"The war had barely started in 1914!" Tommy thundered. "Your poor husband must have been utterly distraught to find that he had married a spy. How did he find out, Miss Cambridge? Did he catch you sending coded messages? Did he overhear you passing on information he had unwittingly shared with you or in your presence?"

"Let us move on." Evelyn forced herself to meet the other woman's furious gaze across the room. "The church that married you has no record of your birth or baptism."

"I wasn't born in Scarborough."

"Where were you born?"

The pause, though infinitesimal, was there. "Nottingham."

"That is a lie." Aunt Em banged her hand on the table. "We have an extremely good contact at Somerset House who confirmed to us today that there has been no child named Clarissa Cambridge born in England within a ten-year timeframe on either side of your purported age."

"You do not know when I was born," Clarissa retorted, but Evelyn could hear the fight leaving the other woman's voice.

"Your age is on your marriage certificate," Evelyn said.

"I told a falsehood, so the age difference between Fred and me didn't look so extreme."

"You"—Tommy pointed at Clarissa to emphasise his point—"are a spy who passed information to the Germans during the war using this school and your marriage as a cover?"

"No," she said weakly, dropping her head into her hands. "No, I didn't. I'm not. I don't understand why you are accusing me of these things."

"Now, Clarissa," Nanny Bunting said as she got to her feet. "Don't let these people bully you with this nonsense about spies and secrets."

"They know." Clarissa started to weep as Nanny Bunting put a hand on her shoulder. "It's all so pointless."

"We know you killed Captain Ralph Gower, young lady," Detective Inspector Andrews said.

For a moment Evelyn wished the detective hadn't spoken, but his unwitting words unleashed a maelstrom of fury in the headmistress's assistant.

"I did not kill anyone," she screeched, hatred filling her voice. "You can hang me as a spy, but I am not a killer."

"Miss Cambridge!" Julia gasped. "How perfectly dreadful. I trusted you."

All eyes were now on the headmistress, who held a trembling hand to her mouth. Her dark eyes shone with tears as she stared in disbelief at her assistant.

Nanny Bunting picked up Clarissa's upturned chair and practically pushed her onto it. "Let us all calm down. You don't know what you're saying, my dear."

"I think she knows perfectly well what she is saying," Tommy said, his voice colder and more biting than the north wind blowing inland off the sea on a winter's day. "She has admitted to being a spy."

"That simply can't be so," Nanny Bunting replied placatingly. "Miss Cambridge has been a pupil here and thereafter a valued member of staff. We would certainly know if her character was in question."

"Who paid her school fees?" Tommy barked out the question.

Nanny Bunting exchanged a sharp glance with Miss Davenport before the latter responded. "We cannot divulge that information."

"I think you will find that you can," Detective Inspector Andrews said sternly. "Either voluntarily or we shall get a court order for every piece of paper in your office. There isn't a judge in the whole of Yorkshire who wouldn't give us access to your records when we tell them what has been going on in your school, Miss Davenport."

Tears streamed down the headmistress's face. "This isn't fair. My school will be destroyed all because of one silly little girl's actions."

"It's rather more serious than that." Tommy's hands balled into fists. He held himself rigid as he addressed Julia Davenport. "A man has been murdered. An oil lamp was thrown into a room, which was then locked in a clear attempt to harm my family. This is about much more than one spy, and you know it."

Julia shook her head. "No, no, I know nothing of the sort. Of course, what happened to Mr Gower was a terrible tragedy, but that should not cause a stain on the name of Docere House."

"What would you say if I told you that *Captain* Gower sought employment here for the explicit purpose of finding out who in this area was passing military secrets to the enemy?" Tommy's words dealt a heavier blow because of the calm, measured way in which he delivered them.

"That's ridiculous." The headmistress held up a handkerchief to her eyes. "That simply isn't true."

The composure of the three women was unravelling in front of their eyes. The only person who seemed relatively in control of herself was Nanny Bunting. Evelyn was gratified to see her plan was working, though there was still much to do.

Tommy could feel his self-control fading as quickly and irrevocably as the sun on a winter's day. Had Julia Davenport not heard Clarissa Cambridge just admitting to being a spy?

"Is it your contention that there has not been a spy ring operating out of your school?"

"A spy ring?" Julia looked up at Tommy. "What a ridiculous assertion."

"And yet your own assistant has just admitted that she is not a murderess but is, in fact, a spy."

"That has nothing to do with my school. Or me."

"How often did Miss Cambridge go home to her family during the school holidays?"

Julia looked at Nanny Bunting for support. "I don't have that information on hand."

"Let me ask you another question, then." Tommy had well and truly got his teeth into questioning the headmistress and was glad no one was interrupting his flow. "Did Miss Cambridge go home to visit her relatives in the six weeks' summer holiday? What about the holiday at Easter? How about last Christmas?"

"She stayed here at the school over the summer," Julia conceded. "I really don't remember what she did over the other holidays. Nor do I see how it's relevant."

"If her family were, for instance, in Germany or some other European country sympathetic to

England's enemy, I'm sure you can see why that would be a cause for concern?"

Julia gave a tight smile. "Well, there's no reason to be concerned, then, is there? I just told you she stayed here all summer."

"You slipped up, you know, when you spoke to me earlier," he said in a conversational tone. "At the time, I was too furious at what you had said to actually analyse the words you used."

"Must I really listen to this?" Julia looked at Detective Inspector Andrews. "Although parents are removing their children in droves, I do still have a school to run."

"Yes, I insist upon it." Two uniformed police officers stood up straighter near the door to the library just in case Julia, or anyone else, thought they had a chance of making a run for it.

"You told me that if Lady Northmoor and myself hadn't gone 'sniffing around in things that do not concern us, then no one would ever have dreamed that Gower's death was anything but a terrible tragedy'. You *wanted* Captain Gower's death to be treated as simple misfortune. You were insistent on that from the moment the police arrived."

"So?" the headmistress lifted a shoulder in defiance. "I thought you were stirring up trouble when there simply wasn't any."

"I don't know how you can say that." Tommy shook his head, the fight leaving him as he despaired of extracting the truth from Julia Davenport. “A man was murdered. You employed a spy at your school. Those things aren’t simply a little bit of trouble—they are a disaster. Hence parents wishing to remove their children immediately.”

“How is your father these days?” Aunt Em asked. “Has he managed to get his gambling addiction under control?”

“Please don’t bring Father into this.” Julia sighed heavily. “He made a terrible mistake a few years back and we will both be eternally grateful to your family for rectifying that wrong.”

“Perhaps your father should be here in the library to answer my question for himself.”

“He’s teaching.” The panicked look from Julia to Nanny Bunting was not missed by anyone in the room. “I beg of you: please don’t involve my father in this mess. He will be utterly mortified.”

Tommy had endured about enough of Julia minimising what had happened at Docere House that day. It seemed she had no wish to accept any responsibility for Ralph’s murder or for employing Clarissa Cambridge as her assistant.

“Who is actually in charge at Docere House?” Evelyn asked. “Is it you, your father, or Nanny Bunting?”

“What a ridiculous question,” Julia said haughtily. “Of course it’s me.”

Nanny Bunting, still standing near Clarissa,

stiffened. Her face twisted into a mask of fury before she visibly took a deep breath and forced herself to relax.

"Even your staff think it's Nanny Bunting who is really the brains, and organisation, behind the heretofore successes of Docere House."

"Whoever said that is quite ridiculous." Julia studiously avoided looking at her secretary. "Nanny has always been very loyal to our family, but she has never had a leadership role."

"And yet it was your former nanny who came up with the solution to get your father out of a particularly sticky betting situation, wasn't it?" As Evelyn asked the question, Tommy watched the look of satisfaction spread over Nanny Bunting's face. He felt invigorated. It was only a matter of time before one of them cracked and turned on the other.

"I don't know what you mean." Julia stared down at the tabletop as her secretary's gaze bore into the back of her head.

"You were desperate when Tommy's Uncle Charles won the school in a bet. I can't imagine how you felt when you realised that, even after that selfish gamble, he had again used the school as a stake in a game of cards."

"He didn't. That did not happen."

"Let us ask him." Evelyn gestured towards the police officers on the door, and they opened it.

Herbert Davenport walked in and looked around the room. "What is going on here?"

"Oh, Daddy." Julia's head drooped in shame and her shoulders shook with sobs.

"Julia, darling? What on earth is wrong?"

"Apologies for the impertinence of this question, sir," Tommy addressed the older man, not relishing what he was about to say. The man was foolish but not a killer, nor unpatriotic. "When you lost the school to my Uncle Charles, did you shortly thereafter make another rather foolish bet?"

It was as though his daughter's embarrassment and clear distress caused Herbert Davenport to take responsibility for his actions. "I did."

"Who with?"

"I don't know who they were," he said. "That is to say, I did not know their names, but I did know *what* they were."

"Which was?"

"Jolly unscrupulous fellows. Loan sharks, to use the vernacular."

"How did you get out of the situation you were in?" Tommy asked. "You had already lost ownership of the school. What did you offer these fellows to satisfy them?"

He looked confused at the question. "I didn't offer them anything."

"Then who did?" Tommy snapped out the question. "Who stopped them from collecting on your debt?"

"Stop!" Julia cried. "Stop it! Please leave him alone."

Tommy allowed the breath he hadn't realised he was holding to leave his body. "We need to get to the truth, Miss Davenport."

"And I shall tell it to you."

"Julia!" Nanny Bunting's warning sounded loudly through the library.

"Nanny Bunting arranged for Father's debt to be repaid. She arranged it all."

"That's quite preposterous." Nanny Bunting's face had twisted into a sneer. "You don't know what you're saying, you silly girl."

Julia lifted her head. "The jig is up, Nanny."

"What did you do?" Herbert asked, his voice pitched only slightly below a wail. "What did you both do?"

"When the villains you owed money to approached me here at the school, I asked Nanny Bunting for help. Of course I did. There's no one I trust more. She said she had an idea, but it would mean putting aside my morals."

"Oh Julia," Herbert moaned. "My dear girl. What did you do?"

"It was the only way to keep the school." Julia gave her father a beseeching look. "You had already lost the school to Charles Christie, but he was allowing us to continue running it for a steep price. The only way to hide that from him was to placate the lowlifes you now owed money to."

"I put you in a terrible position." Herbert shook his head sadly. "But what did you *do*? I simply must know."

Julia swallowed. "I allowed the school to be used in a jolly terrible way. Nanny said it was the only way to save the school. She knew people who would pay a lot of money if we allowed certain people to stay here."

"What people?" Herbert asked, completely baffled.

Tommy felt desperately sorry for the man. He had been a terrible buffoon to allow gambling to consume his life, but he seemed genuinely oblivious to the dreadful lengths his daughter had stooped to.

"Spies." Her voice was muffled by the hand she held over her mouth as though she had finally realised just how appalling her actions had been.

"You allowed my school to be used by spies?" He shook his head as though unable to believe his daughter's words.

"It wasn't your school!" Julia shouted. "You lost it in a card game, remember? I did what I had to do so we were not turned out on our ear. I would do anything for Docere House, you know that. You've always known that."

Herbert staggered and clutched his chest. Detective Sergeant Montgomery sprang forward and caught him before he hit the ground. The older man's face was a hideous shade of grey.

"Daddy!" Julia cried as she rushed from her seat and dropped to the floor next to where the junior detective had rested her father's prostrate body.

Evelyn was too stunned to move. Although her plan for exposing the spy ring at Docere House was working perfectly, she had not foreseen the terrible consequences in front of her. Perhaps she should have known that Herbert Davenport, who was not a young man, could not have withstood the shock of knowing his daughter was complicit in the scheme.

There would be plenty of time for her to examine her accountability later. For now, she simply must push home their advantage, however loathsome it was.

Nanny Bunting left Clarissa Cambridge's side. "I know what to do. Let me help him."

"Don't you touch him!" Julia screamed. "You have done enough. I should never have listened to you."

"Julia, my dear child, I can help him," Nanny Bunting implored. "Please let me help him."

"You are not to touch him." Julia held out a hand

as though to ward her off. "I don't want you near either of us ever again."

"You!" Called Detective Inspector Andrews to one of the uniformed police officers on the door. "Telephone for an ambulance. Tell them to come immediately. Possible heart attack. Also, place a call to the village doctor. There's a chance he will get here sooner and be able to administer aid."

"Please don't die," Julia begged as she cradled her father's head on her lap.

"Miss Davenport"—Evelyn knelt on the floor next to the headmistress— "while I understand this is a terrible time for me to ask, I implore you to tell us the truth."

"What do you want to know?" Julia sobbed.

"Julia, no!" Nanny Bunting tried to drag the headmistress away from her father. Detective Sergeant Montgomery stepped forward and took Nanny Bunting away. He signalled to the remaining police officer, who walked over and placed Nanny Bunting under arrest.

"What are you doing?" she screamed. "You can't do this. You can't arrest me based on the wicked fabrications of these two unhinged young women."

The uniformed officer continued to slowly intone the reasons for her arrest. Detective Inspector Andrews waited until he had finished before he addressed the school secretary. "I never thought that I would have the misfortune to arrest a person such as you. You have breached the Official Secrets Act 1911 and you deserve whatever fate the court sees fit."

"I shall never be found guilty," she said defiantly. "Certainly not on the testimony of those two deranged fools."

The uniformed officer removed Nanny Bunting from the room. Herbert Davenport, although a fearful colour, was still breathing, though his chest rose and fell with a rapidity that was alarming.

"She arranged everything," Julia said in a dull voice as soon as her former nanny had left the room. "She said all I had to do was allow it to happen. I didn't need to be involved. I just had to turn a blind eye."

"You knew that Miss Cambridge was involved?"

"No, not at first." She did not take her gaze from her stricken father. "All I knew was that she was a pupil whose parents lived overseas, so she stayed here rather a lot during holidays."

"But she was just a young girl then," Grace said. "Just a schoolgirl."

"Perhaps she was placed here in England for her own safety." Julia shrugged. "And later she became involved. I don't know. As I told you—I was never involved in how things were run."

"Yet you cannot pretend that you were innocent and above reproach, can you?" Evelyn asked.

"I did a terrible thing." Julia raised her gaze to meet Evelyn's. "But I did it for my father."

"Did you also kill Captain Gower for your father?"

For the smallest moment in time, Evelyn thought Julia would deny her accusation. However, the woman went back to looking at her father. "Everything I did, I did for this school. After Mother died, this place was all Father and I had. It was our *life*. Perhaps we both allowed Docere House to consume us."

"Tell me how it happened. When did you decide he had to die?"

"Clarissa knew he was on to her. She was sure he had seen her either coming out or going into the secret passage. Bertie Adams spoke to me about the deterioration in Gower's concentration and the belief he was carrying out experiments using school equipment on his own time. I went over to the science building late one evening and caught him in the act."

"In the act?" Evelyn frowned.

"He was manufacturing something and, when I asked him what he was doing, he refused to say. At first, I thought it was drugs. The powder, you know. I wondered if he was perhaps making some sort of illicit drugs to sell. So I watched him. Clarissa watched him. Nanny watched him. We saw him go out on his walks. Crucially, we saw him visit the yew tree on many occasions and leave with berries, bark, and sometimes leaves."

"So when he thought he was being followed, he actually was?" Tommy's voice vibrated with anger as he asked the question.

"Yes, he wasn't going mad. He wasn't paranoid. We were watching him."

"And then?" Evelyn looked at Tommy as she directed her query to Julia, the pain on his face almost too much for her to see.

"One day when he was teaching, Nanny and I searched the laboratory until we found the powder. By then, of course, we had worked out he was making taxine. He had to be stopped."

"*You* poisoned him?" Tommy asked in disgust.

"He trusted me. I offered him a cup of coffee when he came to see me about his concerns regarding Edwin Miller's teaching."

"And the attack in the library?"

"I knew what you were both like when Charles and Eddie were killed. I knew you would stop at nothing."

"Your plan was to kill us?"

"Of course not," Julia said, sounding outraged for the first time. "I wanted to scare you enough to make you go home and leave us all alone."

"To be clear, Miss Davenport," Detective Inspector Andrews said, "you threw a lit oil lamp onto the rug in the library?"

"Yes," she whispered, then raised her gaze to his. "I know you must arrest me. Of course I know that. But I beg you to show me some mercy. Please allow me to go to the hospital with my father."

"How much mercy did you show your victim?" Tommy asked. "How much mercy did you show Captain Gower when you poisoned him to death?"

Julia hung her head and refused to answer his question. For her, the jig was most definitely up.

14

"I know I say this every time," Aunt Em said. "But I'm afraid there are still some parts I simply don't understand."

"What do you need help with?" Tommy asked. Although he still felt extremely sad about the needless death of Ralph Gower, he was glad that they had extracted a confession from his killer and put an end to the spy ring that had been operating in his home county.

"How did you know Miss Cambridge was the spy, but didn't kill Captain Gower?"

"Ralph told us that the spy was a woman. We were told he had been arguing with Miss Cambridge and had warned Francis Galbraith away from her, calling her dangerous. Of course, we were also told that he had made a comment about national security to Miss Davenport, which suggested he'd spoken to her about the issue.

Evelyn took up the narrative. "We knew Clarissa couldn't have poisoned Ralph. He knew she was the spy. Therefore, there was no way he would have accepted a drink from her. The person who poisoned him must have been someone he trusted."

"Do you think Captain Gower deliberately got a job at Docere House to find the spy? Do you think it was a dangerous mission that he undertook without fear for his life?" These questions were asked rather enthusiastically by Grace.

"We shall never know," Tommy told his youngest sister indulgently. "It's not as though the government will let the truth be known, but his last letter certainly seems to suggest that's what happened. There will probably be brave men up and down the country, as well as abroad, doing similar work to Captain Gower in an attempt to rid this country of spies and help to keep it safe from our enemies."

"What about Somerset House?" Constance asked with a slight frown. "You said we had found information about Clarissa's birth. Well, specifically that there hadn't been a child named Clarissa Cambridge, born in England. That wasn't true, was it?"

"We didn't have time to ask my friend," Aunt Em said. "So I'm afraid I fibbed."

"Aunt Em!" Constance suppressed a laugh. "That wasn't a fib. It was an outright lie!"

"Well maybe so," Aunt Em said primly. "But it was for the good of the country, so completely acceptable."

Any other thoughts—final clarification?

"Where are we going?" Grace asked as she trailed along behind Tommy and Evelyn, with Constance at her side.

"You shall see," Evelyn said with a smile.

When they reached the stables, Evelyn beckoned them inside the stall where the kittens were playing in a shaft of late-afternoon sunlight. Tommy picked up the black kitten with the white patch over his eye and snuggled him into his chest.

"They are extremely sweet." Grace got on the floor, and immediately the kitten jumped into her lap. "Are we taking them home? Please say we are."

"We are," Evelyn confirmed. "I believe they may need someone to check on their wellbeing frequently. Perhaps someone to play with them."

"I would do that," Grace said immediately. "Please, may I? I would take excellent care of them."

"Of course you may," Evelyn responded. "Constance?"

Her elder sister-in-law eyed her with horror. "No. Grace can do it. I can't imagine getting down on a dusty floor or cleaning up after them. Though, I must say, they are jolly pretty."

"We need names for them." Tommy looked at Grace. "If you are going to take responsibility for them, it only seems fair that you name them."

"Well, that's simple." Grace grinned up at her family. "Sherlock and Watson—what else?"

EPILOGUE

Some weeks later, Tommy sought out Evelyn and found her, unsurprisingly enough, in the nursery.

Evelyn sat in the rocking chair, a sleeping Isabelle nuzzling into her mother's neck. Tommy thought he'd never seen anything quite so beautiful in his life.

"What is it?" She asked, one hand on Isabelle's back, the other outstretched to meet his.

"I've received a letter from Herbert Davenport."

"He's alive?" Surprise sounded clearly in her voice. "Goodness me. I wasn't expecting that. I still feel terribly guilty about what happened to him."

"You have nothing to feel guilty about," he assured her. "Herbert's heart attack is not something we could have foreseen."

"Where is he now?"

"He's in a sanitorium."

"Does he mention Julia?"

"He does not," Tommy said grimly. "At least not by name. He does, however, apologise for his role in what happened and says he bears the full responsibility himself."

"Well, that's ridiculous," Evelyn retorted. "Obviously his actions were extremely selfish and beyond foolhardy, but Nanny Bunting and Clarissa Cambridge would have found some way to operate with or without Herbert Davenport's poor choices."

"I agree."

"What does the letter say? You look jolly pensive."

"He says he expects to live out the rest of his life at the sanitorium and intends to transfer Docere House back to me. He says he never should have allowed me to gift it back to him after Uncle Charles died."

"Goodness me, Tommy. Whatever will you do with a school?"

"I do have some ideas." He sat in the chair next to Evelyn. "Perhaps you would like to hear about them?"

"I most certainly would."

"First, I intend to provide Herbert with a small pension so he may live comfortably wherever he chooses. Second, I will create a scholarship in Ralph's name. I would intend this grant to be for the use of children of men who have served in the military—to give them a chance of an education they otherwise would not receive."

"Boys and *girls*?"

"Of course," he answered, as though the question was a silly one. "Why would I want less for other people's daughters than I want for my own?"

"What else?"

"Well, I shall need some sort of committee to appoint the money to worthy causes on a yearly basis."

"Ah," Evelyn said. "This is where I come into your little scheme, isn't it?"

"Subject to your approval, and you all agreeing, I would like to appoint you, my darling, Aunt Victoria, Millie, Isolde, and Grace to the board of the school. You will decide how the school is run, and who will receive the Ralph Gower scholarship."

Tears filled Evelyn's eyes. "Aunt Victoria and Millie and the most organised women I have ever met. Isolde has a background in education, and serving on the board will give Grace a purpose she is currently lacking. I, of course, would be honoured to serve, particularly in Ralph's name."

Tommy lifted Evelyn's hand and pressed a kiss into her palm. "I can't think of more suitable women to fulfil the role."

"Aunt Victoria and Millie may clash horribly. They are both extremely opinionated."

"After Constance and Alexander's wedding, Aunt Victoria will need something to fill her time. Millie's children can all be educated at Docere House if that is something she and Reggie want. I know private education is not in their budget, given Reggie's salary as a general practitioner."

"You seem to have thought of everything." Evelyn smiled lovingly at her husband. "I think Millie will be thrilled that you thought of her."

"It will join our families together even more closely than they already are. And I think you are wrong. I don't believe Aunt Victoria and Millie will clash, but instead, I consider they will become extremely fond of each other."

"You are an extremely clever man, Thomas Christie."

"Of course I am, my dearest darling," he replied. "I married you, didn't I?"

ACKNOWLEDGMENTS

I researched the role of spies during World War 1 extensively before writing this book. While I have tried to make this aspect of *Murder at Docere House* as realistic as possible, I have occasionally used artistic license to advance the plot. For example, although there was a German Navy attack on Scarborough in December 1914, I do not know if specific information about the whereabouts of the British Navy at that time was passed to the Germans by a spy.

My grateful thanks to my brother-in-law, David Leaming, for his guidance on Navy ranks. Any mistakes I may have made in the information he gave me (in very good faith!), or in my understanding of my research for this book, are, of course, my own.

ABOUT THE AUTHOR

Born in Germany to a military father, Catherine's early years were an adventure in themselves. For the first 14 years of her life, she called various countries abroad her home. It was during this time that she developed her insatiable appetite for stories, courtesy of her school library.

With each turn of the page, Catherine became captivated by two genres: romance and mysteries. The daring escapades of Nancy Drew left a mark on her, igniting a love for mystery stories. Soon, she discovered the genius of Agatha Christie, whose books remain her favourites to this day.

Catherine's bestselling Tommy & Evelyn Christie Mysteries transport readers to the North Yorkshire countryside of the 1920s while the Martha Miller Mysteries unfold in the charming countryside of post-World War 2 Berkshire. Catherine's new series, the West Cliffe Bay Cosy Mysteries are contemporary mysteries set in a fictional North Yorkshire village.

Catherine shares her home with her youngest

child and two delightfully spoiled dogs who have no idea they are not human.

Want to join the fun? Click here to join Catherine's newsletter and here to join Catherine's Facebook reader group.

Manufactured by Amazon.ca
Bolton, ON

46811725R00148